MARSHMALLOWS

Wanda Collins

Contents

Prologue

~ Prologue ~

~  ~

"I order you to kiss my brother."

I knew what my best friend was going to say before the words left her mouth. I should have known she was planning something when we made our bet on the two boys with us. Reyna's brother and boyfriend were playing a fighting video game, so we thought it would be fun to stake on who would be the victor. The loser of the bet would have to follow through with one demand from the winner.

This is what I get for thinking her stupid brother could beat her genius boyfriend.

"What?!" Ian shouted, staring wide-eyed at his sister. "What is this about, Reyna?"

Reyna was dropping hints for quite a while that she knew about my feelings towards Ian, but I wasn't even sure how I truly felt about him anymore. A childhood crush was just that; nothing but a naive crush on a boy who never noticed me. I thought I had mostly grown out of it, but the opportunity to kiss the boy I had once been crazy about seemed too good to pass up.

"She lost a bet," Reyna told him. Then she looked at me and said, "It can be on the cheek or nose. Or just the back of his hand."

I couldn't figure out if she was challenging me or trying to take some of the pressure off. Knowing my best friend so well, it was probably a combination of the two.

"Reyns, stop. She doesn't have to--"

"Shut up," I cut him off. I was weighing the pros and cons in my head and he was making it difficult to concentrate.

It wasn't like he never kissed a girl before, so it wouldn't even mean anything to him. I've also had my fair share of kisses, so I could treat it the same way. Nothing would have to change between us. It was no big deal. Just one kiss. Right?

"I was only trying to help! It's just a stupid bet. You don't have to do it," he told me before turning back to Reyna. "Seriously, Reyns! Are you crazy?"

He couldn't just be quiet for two seconds! Without thinking, I gripped his collar and yanked him closer until we were only inches apart. "I said shut up! I am trying to think, you obnoxious idiot!"

His response was a weak, "Okay."

I closed my eyes as I reached a decision. I wasn't going to get another chance and I couldn't deny that I wanted to do it at least once in my life. So I opened my eyes and leaned in before I changed my mind. It was awkward because we kept our gazes locked on each other. I could see the flash of surprise when he realized my lips were on his, but it was gone as quickly as the kiss was over.

A moment lapsed between us. My fist tightened around the cotton fabric of his shirt as we both leaned in, neither of us fully comprehending what we were doing when our eyes closed and our lips met a second time. His were soft and warm against mine, but the kiss was chaste. I knew I was holding back, but it strangely seemed as if Ian was too. His hands barely grazed my waist as he hesitated to do more. That was when I broke the kiss and let go of his wrinkled shirt to shove him away.

From the corner of my eye, I noticed he was a little off balance from me shoving him. Or maybe because of me? I wondered as I quickly turned away from everyone to take a deep breath and compose myself.

I just kissed my best friend's brother in front of my best friend and her boyfriend. The very thought made my head spin, adding to my fluster. Only the determination to get revenge allowed me to face them again.

With a grin, I asked Reyna, "Why don't you tell your brother what you two," I gestured to her and Wesley, "get up to in that supply closet?"

The vengeance I sought not only got back at Reyna who was finding it all so amusing until now, but it also distracted Ian from what just happened between us. He was way overprotective of his little sister and I took full advantage of it for the situation.

The supply closet was more like a small chemistry lab and they mostly studied in there. They had to have made out once or twice though. I knew I would if I was in Reyna's neon shoes. Not with Wesley, of course. Ew. Maybe with someone like...

Just as I glanced at Ian, he released the shrillest tone I had ever heard. My six-year-old sister couldn't even hit that range.

"Supply closet?!"

Reyna inched behind Wesley to hide from her livid brother. I did enjoy watching him get all riled up because it was always entertaining, but I never failed to rescue my bestie. Wesley can fend for himself, I thought as I watched Reyna step in front of Wesley and make up an excuse for him to leave the room.

"You better run, you four-eyed casanova!" Ian shouted as Wesley ran upstairs.

For being a guest in Wesley's house, Ian wasn't treating him very well. They didn't really get along anyway because Ian was so concerned about his little sister and didn't want her to get hurt. Wesley appeared to have enough respect for Ian to put up with his dramatic behavior, but Ian couldn't see it.

The doorbell rang, so Reyna ran out of the room to answer it and get the pizza we ordered and left me all alone with the smoking beefcake. Really, I thought I saw smoke coming off of his blonde head from all of his fuming.

"Alright, loser. Let's vent some of that anger on the game. I'll even let you win," I said, patting his shoulder and sitting back down on the couch.

Ian looked at me then and blinked before he scanned the room, realizing it was just the two of us. He cleared his throat and sat beside me on the very edge of the seat.

I rolled my eyes and put my arm across his chest to push him back against the couch. Then I tossed a controller onto his lap and waited for him to choose a character. After a tentative glance my way, Ian picked up the controller and selected the character he created of himself. It looked just like him with blonde hair and green eyes, but the character was herculean and wielding giant mallet. I chose the one I created too; A slender girl with dirty blonde hair who's fighting style resembled dancing.

A minute into the match, he was struggling to stay alive as he muttered, "I thought you said you would let me win, Ferret."

I held back a smile at his nickname for me. Even though I typically hated him for still using the name that haunted me in elementary and middle school, it held a certain amount of normalcy that we both needed after our liplock.

"You're cheating!" Ian accused.

"How am I cheating, huh? Just because I don't button-mash like you does not make me a cheater."

He cursed when I did a special attack and knocked his character out of the ring.

"See?" I grinned at him before the second round started, "I never cheat. I'm just really good at kicking your ass."

He turned to me then and said under his breath, "You're cheating right now with that smile."

The controller dropped from my hands and I hurried to pick it back up when I saw him crushing my idle character.

"Now that is cheating," I muttered, dancing around him and fighting back with all of my tricks.

I was curious if things were in fact back to normal because of his typical shameless flirting. Then when I won the second battle, he started sulking in his poor loser ways and I took it as a good sign.

In the short silence before the final match, we heard Wesley and Reyna talking to someone and the front door close. Since they would be back any minute, I tried to draw out the fight so we wouldn't have an awkward silence to fill.

"They're being too quiet," he stated as I continued to dodge or block him.

"Maybe they're making out." I smirked because that was most likely what they were doing in the entryway, but the timing of my comment was bad because I delivered the final blow right after I said it.

My smile fell when I realized Ian was staring at me with the expression of a deer caught in the headlights. He glanced at my lips, causing my brows to raise at the subtle action and his to drop as he quickly looked away.

I jumped when he yelled to Wesley, "Black! I demand a rematch. And if you're making out with my sister, I'll go buy a real mallet."

I snorted at his threat and stood up when they came into the room. Stepping over to Reyna after Wesley sat down at a safe distance from Ian, I whispered to her, "Sorry, I tried to keep him busy. It just didn't take long for me to beat him."

Reyna laughed and thanked me. I was going to keep the thought of them making out that I planted in Ian's mind a secret. There was no need to start a revenge war with my best friend, and I knew she would come up with something to pay me back if she found out about it. It would undoubtedly involve Ian too.

Ian cheerfully welcomed him back into the living room. "Now let's have a talk about that supply closet, shall we?"

"Seriously?" Wesley pointed at me and said, "She just kissed you and you're going to forget it?"

He was making a second enemy out of me.

"You can interrogate me anytime. I assume Ferra kissing you doesn't happen every day."

I bit the inside of lip to keep my jaw from dropping as he dug a deeper grave for himself. I fixed him with my best glare and he was smart enough to look nervous.

"No, I'm not going to forget it!" My attention snapped to Ian and he looked at me. "Not that it meant anything...?" I didn't respond and kept a blank face, making him more desperate to get it right. "Or maybe it did?"

I loved that I had the ability to unnerve him so much. No matter how he felt about me, he was affected by our kiss in some way and that alone made it worth losing the bet. I felt powerful. It was like learning about him owning a pair of sparkly vampire boxers all over again, only this was even better. I could tease him in an entirely different way now.

I sighed lightly, making myself comfortable on the floor. I leaned back on my hands and tilted my head, watching him squirm. Ian jumped to his feet and announced that he was going to get some water from the kitchen. Reyna laughed hysterically, so I reached my foot out and kicked her.

It wasn't until much later that the four of us settled in to watch a movie. Ian and I were back on the couch, forcing the cuddling couple to lay on the floor in front of us. For me, it was wanting to curl up on the comfortable cushions. For Ian, it was to ensure all hands remained in sight during the movie. Wesley and Reyna didn't care in the slightest because they just ignored him.

Ian was being more awkward with me than before, if that was even possible. I was starting to get tired of my little game and just wanted the adorable idiot to be himself again. At least it didn't take long for us to get absorbed in the plot of what we were watching and I pushed the events of our evening to the back of my mind.

Towards the middle of the movie, I stretched my legs out over Ian's lap. It was something I had done for years whenever we shared a couch, so I thought nothing of it in my distracted state. Ian choking on some popcorn caught my attention. He was fine after a drink of water, but I suddenly became self-conscious of my habit. My heart sank at the thought of him not being comfortable with it anymore.

"Sorry." I started to pull my legs back to my own space on the couch.

Keeping his eyes on the screen, he reached out and wrapped his fingers around my ankles to stop me from moving farther away. "It's fine," he mumbled and pulled them back over his lap.

I smiled, curling my toes when his hands stayed where they were and returned my focus to the movie.

By the time the movie was over, Ian was acting much more like himself. He perked up at the mention of a waterpark in Reyna's and my discussion of our summer plans. The season was coming up in a couple of weeks, so we were excited to start it off in a big way.

"Why am I hearing about this for the first time?" Ian asked me when Wesley and Reyna started talking.

"Because not all of our plans involve you."

"Well, now that I know about it, I'm going with you guys," he crossed his arms.

"No. Your germs will contaminate the pools."

He scoffed in offense, "My germs will only improve the quality of the water. Everyone can swim in my sexiness."

I slapped my forehead with my palm. "Do you hear yourself when you speak?"

"It will be like the Fountain of Youth except it's the Pool of Ian. With a water slide."

I covered my ears. "Oh, my god. Shut up!"

He spoke loud enough for me to hear, "Not until you say I can go!"

"Fine!" I conceded. "Just take a shower before we leave."

"Why bother when I'm going to a water park? I can get a free shower there."

"You can get a free shower at home too!"

"Not true," he held a finger up. "There is such a thing as a water bill, you know."

I groaned into my hands, wondering why I had any semblance of feelings for Ian Winters at any point in my life.

It's going to be a long summer.

1 | Water Balloons

1 | Water Balloons

A giggle that sounded far too evil woke me from my dream of dancing with Channing Tatum in his Step Up days.

"Go away, Megan," I grumbled, burying my head under a pillow.

"But it's the first day of summer!" I heard my best friend's voice accompanied with a cheer from my little sister. "Sunshine," Reyna addressed Megan, "I think it's time for a Ferra-pile."

I threw the blanket aside and rolled off of my bed, which was a far better alternative than being crushed. "Don't you dare."

"And she's up!" Reyna gave Meg a high five and sent her off to the kitchen for breakfast.

I rubbed my eyes to clear the sleep out of them since I obviously wouldn't be getting more of it. Reyna's bright tank top blinded me so I had to look away. It was too early for such vibrant colors and she had three sources with her top, the straps from the swimsuit she wore underneath, and her sandals. At least her blue jean shorts toned down the outfit. The sun was too bright for the morning too, but a certain someone opened my curtains.

"Get dressed," she ordered. "Ian is waiting outside. It's time to initiate Operation: H2O Attack on Wesley Black."

"I hope that's a working title," I muttered, searching for some clothes in my closet.

"Nope. I spent all night on that one," she admitted proudly.

I rolled my eyes and smiled while pulling a simple one-piece swimsuit off of its hanger. Then followed that with a loose-fitting scoop neck white shirt. I spent most of last night unpacking my summer clothes for the warm season and stuffing my cold weather clothes into the back of my closet.

"Skit?" I called Reyna by the nickname I gave her years ago due to her obsession with Skittles.

"Yes, Ferra?"

"Get out."

"I'm out," she held her hands up and backed away. "Bring a change of clothes. We're taking Wes shopping for swim trunks afterwards. He doesn't have any for our trip to the water park next week."

After she was gone, I grabbed a pair of leggings and made a small pile on my bed for the second outfit.

I quickly changed and put my hair up in a bun. I wanted to try to protect it from getting completely soaked, but it was unlikely to stay dry. Checking myself in the mirror, I gave my reflection a nod of approval before going to brush my teeth.

I didn't usually care so much about my appearance, but I found myself wanting to show off a little around Ian. After that kiss, nothing changed between us. Deep, deep...deep down, that kind of bothered me because it meant that he wasn't so affected by me anymore. And he damn well should have been playing it on repeat in his thick skull for months since my lips graced his and he was not worthy.

Otherwise, I was happy to spend the summer with our relationship the same as it had always been; him, the annoying big brother of my best friend, and me, the snarky best friend of his little sister who picked on him. Unfortunately, along with that came the usual flutter of anticipation whenever I knew I was going to see him. That was something that never really went away, so I was used to it by now.

I went into the kitchen to tell my parents where I was going and that I would be home later. They were busy eating breakfast and denying Meg ice cream for her meal, but their attention turned to me when they said to have fun.

"I get to throw water balloons at my bestie's boyfriend and Ian," I grinned. "I will most definitely be having fun."

"Ten points for hitting Ian in the face!" My dad called out as I walked to the front door.

My family was well-acquainted with Reyna's family because we've been friends for so long. My mom was close to Reyna's mom, and my dad got along with her too. Ian was a different story, but it wasn't his fault nor mine that my dad caught a glimpse of my dairy when I was twelve years old. I never left it open on my desk again after that little incident.

I could only be grateful that he didn't say anything to Ian about it or give him the same lecture he gave to me. It involved bats and wasps--the supposed less-friendly versions of birds and bees--and ended with the wasps being eaten. To this day, I didn't think he knew what he was talking about and I didn't either.

"No!" Meg cried. She had a crush on Ian. And Wesley. And any other remotely attractive guy who gave her attention. I pitied her for when she would get to learn all about bats and wasps. "Not Mr. Glitter's face!"

I laughed at my little sister's nickname for Ian, all because I told her about his sparkly vampire boxers as revenge for him sharing my awful nickname with her. Closing the door to the chaos inside, I took a breath of fresh air. The sun had only just risen and the air was still crisp from a cool night. I yawned, slinging my bag over my shoulder and dragged my feet to Ian's red truck at the end of the driveway.

When I climbed inside, I ordered, "You guys are buying my coffee. It is way too early for this mission, Skit. Unless you plan to freeze his ass off too."

"Don't talk about any man's ass in front of me, please. Especially one involved with my sister," Ian cringed from the driver's seat as he backed out onto the street.

"I could just talk about yours then," I said lightly. "Like how flat it is..."

He seemed to perk up when he asked, "You've been looking?"

"You just admitted that it's flat," I countered quickly instead of answering. Of course I was guilty of an occasional glance, because whether I liked him or not, I could still admire his assets.

Ian bristled, "It is not!"

"Pancakes."

"What?" He was confused like I changed the subject. "You want pancakes and coffee? I'm not made of money, you know."

I snorted, though Reyna outright laughed at him missing the comparison.

"Oh my dear, sweet brother," she shook her head and patted his shoulder. "You are so stupid."

"I don't get it. What did I miss?"

She and I started giggling together.

Once we had our fill of caffeine and pancakes, we were all ready to set our plan into motion and parked down the street from Wesley's house.

His mom was in on it, so she gave us free reign of their water to fill the balloons and water guns which were all in the back of the truck. We carried everything to the side of the house, staying out of sight from his window in case he woke up.

It took us nearly a half an hour to fill all of the balloons and tie them. By the time we were done, there were four full buckets of ammunition and the water guns were fully loaded. Two guns and one bucket of balloons for each of us, including Wesley since it wouldn't be a fair fight if he didn't have any weapons.

The three of us took our positions behind the bushes near the front door. Reyna was on one side with her ammo, while Ian and I were crouched on the other side with ours. She gave us a thumbs up after calling his mom to tell her we were ready. His mom's role was to wake him up and send him out to the grocery store.

Then came the waiting.

"He better hurry," I grumbled with the mulch digging into my knees through the thin fabric. There would be splinters to deal with when we were done.

Ian was huddled beside me, so he could see my discomfort. He tugged gently on my arm, moving back as he pulled me towards his spot and traded places with me. My knees landed on the soft, cool grass once I got readjusted and brush off my legs.

"Thanks," I whispered. Despite his extreme case of ignorance, Ian was the sweetest guy I had ever known. He often showed it in small gestures like that and I had to give him that he could be observant every once in a while.

Ian nodded, sparing me a glance before focusing back on the front door. He was eager to pelt his sister's boyfriend with water balloons.

"I guess you do have the ability to be a gentleman...sometimes." I muttered with a smirk. It was the equivalent of poking a bear--or more specifically, a teddy bear--with a stick. I knew exactly how to get a reaction out of him and draw his attention to me.

He scoffed, turning to face me. "I'm always a gentleman. You just don't appreciate me."

"I could give you a few examples of when you were the exact opposite of a gentleman," I said, ready to list off my observations.

"Ok, maybe not always," Ian agreed. Then he smiled, "But I am always nice to you."

I blinked, not entirely sure how to respond. I couldn't think of any time when he was a jerk to me and, if anything, I was the one that wasn't so nice to him. We could throw snarky or teasing comments at each other nonstop, but I was having difficulty coming up with a retort for once.

I took an interest in the door, wishing that it would open and spare me. I shrugged one shoulder after a long pause, "So what? You're nice to every girl."

He cleared his throat and from the corner of my eye, I saw that he was staring at the door again too. I fought back a grin at his silence. It may not have been the best, but my response still managed to stump him.

Only then did Wesley Black decide to grace us with his presence.

Reyna's warrior cry was our cue to begin our attack. Ian and I stood up right after she did across from us. She and I started spraying Wesley with water guns while Ian pelted him with the balloons.

Wesley jumped at our sudden appearance. Using his arms to protect his face from being hit, he stood there and took it all because there was no cover and he couldn't go back into the house. We stopped when he was soaking wet from head to toe.

Reyna ran over to give him a hug. "Good morning, Wes!"

He chuckled quietly and wrapped his arms around her. "Good morning."

I smiled, watching the two of them share a sweet kiss. I counted down from three under my breath, knowing that their moment was going to be ruined.

"Break it up, loverboy!" Ian shouted just as I got to one and he aimed for the side of Wesley's head.

'Loverboy' blocked it and the balloon burst on his arm, splashing onto both him and Reyna.

"Hello, Ian," Wesley greeted him dryly. "Ferra," he added with more cheerfulness since I wasn't the one who interrupted the kiss.

"Are you ready for the best summer ever?" Reyna asked him.

He wasn't very social in school until Reyna came along, so it was the first summer in who knew how long that he would spend with friends.

It was also a big summer for Ian, since he took a gap year before college and it was nearly over. While he was going to spare some time for his other friends, he decided to invade in most of our plans. I was happy that he would be around because I wouldn't feel like a third wheel to Reyna and Wesley. That, and the countless times I was bound to see Ian without a shirt on; I could never complain about getting a little eye candy.

"Ferret," Ian murmured, snapping me out of my thoughts.

I kept my voice low while the other two were talking. "What?"

"You thinking what I'm thinking?"

I highly doubted we were both thinking about how delicious he looked shirtless, but he did have quite the ego so maybe it was true. Then I realized what he meant as his eyes danced from them to the water arsenal. I nodded, discreetly reaching into my bucket of balloons and filling my arms with them.

Ian picked up both of his loaded water guns and positioned them for firing on the unsuspecting couple.

He whispered, "Ready?"

"Let's do it, pretty boy," I grinned and threw the first balloon at Reyna's back. Sorry, Skit. All is fair in love and water wars.

She shrieked and yanked Wesley behind the shrubbery for cover while we relentlessly fired at them.

The battle began and we stayed as two teams. Our initial plan was girls vs boys, but Ian practically begged me to stay on his side so he wouldn't have to work with Wes.

They were in the front yard, while Ian and I had the backyard. During a lull while we waited for them to strike, Ian insisted that we needed a name since they already had one.

"If they're Team Reyley, we could be," he stopped to consider. "Team Fian? Or Ferran?"

"No," I shook my head, despite the tiny leap my heart made. "We're not a ship."

His brows furrowed, "Huh?"

Like I would explain that to him. I tried once to define ships and ship names to him, but I wasn't about to do it again with the two of us as the example.

Instead I proclaimed my first thought, "Team Glitter Ferret!"

Before he could protest, the sprinklers turned on and startled us. Water shot at us from all directions, the cheap tactic distracting us as the cheaters appeared with water balloons.

An hour was spent on ambushes and standoffs, some of them were strategic while others consisted of running and laughing like hyenas with a lot of aimless shooting. By the end of it, there were no distinct winners and left us all exhausted and soggy.

Wesley's mom threw out some towels for us to dry off after we wrung out our sopping clothes, then she allowed us inside to change for our trip to the mall. When it was my turn in the bathroom, I peeled my clothes off and slipped into a pair of dry shorts and a tee. I let my hair down and towel-dried the wet tips before pulling it into a high ponytail so it wouldn't get frizzy. I was the last to join the others outside, just behind Reyna.

"So you want to follow us, Black?" Ian asked him as he twirled his keys on his finger.

"We can all fit in your truck, Ian," Reyna said, looping her hand through her boyfriend's arm.

She was crazy. We would all be squished together because there was no backseat. Unless one or two sat in the bed of the pickup truck, but when I saw her flash an innocent smile, I had a bad feeling that wasn't part of her plan. It was too long of a drive for that too, so it didn't make any sense.

Ian rolled his eyes and muttered to himself, getting into the driver's seat. He wasn't too happy about it either, but I imagined it had more to do with specifically the two of them in such close quarters. I would kill him if made me sit between the couple just to keep them apart, not that I would ever allow that to happen in the first place.

"What are you plotting?" I whispered to my friend with a narrowed gaze.

"Nothing!" She sighed when I pursed my lips. "Don't be so suspicious of your bestie."

"Don't do things that make me suspicious of my bestie," I countered quietly. "Seriously, if you guys want to be together, just follow us over in his car. I assumed that's what we were going to do anyway."

She just smiled at me. I glanced over at Wesley and he was at least attempting to hide his, but it was obvious that he was in on it too. If their plan was to annoy Ian, I was all for it, but I highly doubted it was for that reason. Either way, I supposed I could enjoy the show while being crushed against the passenger door.

Just as she opened the door to get in first, Reyna came to an abrupt halt.

"Oh, Wes. I forgot my, um, sunglasses in your house. Will you come with me to find them?"

"Yeah," he readily agreed to go. "Since they could be anywhere."

Did she even have sunglasses? I wondered as she told me they would be right back. I scoffed at the backs of their scheming selves and climbed into the truck.

"Where did they run off to?" Ian asked me.

"Oh, you know. Probably off to have a quick make out sesh before we go."

"What?!" He unbuckled his seatbelt to go after them.

"Chill," I laughed, taking such joy in teasing him. "It was a joke. They're not gonna do anything in front of his mom..."

Don't say it, Ferra.

He relaxed.

Don't do it.

I couldn't resist.

"Unless they go to his bedroom."

Just as he opened the door to barge in after them, they came out of the house holding hands. Ian slammed the door shut and buckled up again.

"She was just getting her sunglasses," I assured him as I caught sight of the shades in her other hand. Maybe she wasn't lying?

I felt stupid when they climbed in because her motive was clear as I was forced to move over for them. I was sandwiched between Ian and Reyna, while Wesley had my coveted window seat. I had no choice but to sit with one leg on either side of the console. Which in itself was not a problem, but Ian's truck was manual.

I glared at my best friend and she hid behind a pair of sunglasses that most definitely did not belong to her. She had to have borrowed them from Wesley or his mother. They may have hid her shifting eyes, but nothing could hide that guilty smile.

Ian started the truck in a huff, upset and distracted with the thoughts I put in his head. He looked ready to kick his sister's boyfriend out just because of what I said about them making out. I would have felt bad for Wesley, but he was conspiring with Reyna against me. The engine rumbled to life and Ian reached for the stick shift. All the anger left his body as he finally took notice of the situation.

I watched on in humiliation as his eyes went to my bare leg, which not only was between him and the stick shift, but also pressed up against his leg. He hesitated to reach over me and I tried my best to act casual, but I couldn't even look at him.

"Excuse me, Ferret," he said after a moment, his voice as tight as our space. Then he shifted the truck into first gear.

His forearm grazed my inner thigh every time he needed to shift gears. There was tension not only in his muscles but his entire body as he moved almost robotically. He tried to be respectful by holding his arm out uncomfortably, but I couldn't let him do that through the whole drive. When he shifted again, I pushed his arm down to rest on my leg. The action caused the truck to lurch forward, but Ian smoothed it out and mumbled an apology.

I would have grinned at the effect I had on him and even go so far as to call him out on it if I wasn't just as tense. Sitting back as far as I could on the wide bench seat with my feet tucked in on the floorboards, I sat as still as a statue. My stomach flipped in not exactly an unpleasant way whenever his arm moved, but my heart was beating out of my chest the entire time. I considered myself lucky to be able to maintain steady breathing, if not a little shallow.

It had to be the longest drive of my life until we pulled into the parking lot of the mall. Ian went for the first available spot and practically fell out of the truck in his rush to create some distance. I couldn't blame him since I felt an overwhelming sense of relief when

I got out too. Kissing the ground wouldn't have been overdramatic at that point, but I refrained from doing it.

"Well, that was a fun trip," Reyna commented lightly.

She linked her arm with Wesley's once again as they made their way towards the entrance. Ian and I shared an awkward glance and looked away before following behind them, dragging our feet every step of the way.

We did not agree with her.

2 | Sunglasses

2 | Sunglasses

~ ☁ ☀ ☁ ~

On the list of what I love most, shopping was right up there with dancing and mocha frappes.

Especially when it involved torturing and humiliating boys with Reyna.

"Can't I just get the black pair?" Wesley muttered as he nudged his glasses higher onto his nose.

Reyna pouted at him, holding a hanger up. "But I can get a black swimsuit and if you get these, it's like wearing each other's colors."

He scowled at the bright swim trunks, "Why does your color have to be rainbow?"

I threw my arm around her shoulders. "Because she's obsessed with Skittles. To think," I looked at her, "Wesley Black doesn't want to see his girl wearing a sexy black bikini."

"Nothing sexy!" Ian voiced a little too loudly, earning a dirty look from a nearby shopper. He was leaning against the wall, arms crossed as he glared over at us with an expression of irritation and boredom.

I waved him off and turned my attention back to Wesley, giving him an expectant stare as we waited for him to make a choice. His eyes bounced from me to Reyna as he considered what I said and when his gaze lingered on her for a long moment, I knew we succeeded in convincing him.

"Fine." With a resigned sigh, he took the shorts and told her, "I'll do it for you."

"Uh huh," I grinned, getting a stab in my ribs courtesy of my best friend's elbow. It was rightfully deserved after I made her blush and Wesley thoroughly uncomfortable. I knew for a fact after interrogating Reyna that her boyfriend wasn't so shy when he was alone with her, but it was adorable to see them both so flustered. I needed to get some sort of revenge for the seating arrangement in the truck, so my mission was accomplished.

It was only fair to shift the humiliation onto someone else now. It would be wrong to leave him out and--being the nice person that I am--I couldn't allow that to happen.

Skimming through the men's swimwear, I spotted the perfect item for what I had in mind. Humming to myself, I plucked the hanger from the rack and hid it behind my back.

"Hey, Ian."

He glanced over at me. "What?"

"I found the perfect thing for you to wear to the waterpark."

A skeptic brow rose as he asked, "You did, did you?"

Nodding eagerly, I revealed the piece of clothing to everyone. I heard Reyna cackling while I waved it in front of Ian and watched his face fall.

He was not impressed with the gold, glittering speedo.

I could be mean, but I wasn't heartless. After a good laugh at his expense, I put the skimpy bottoms back where they came from and picked out a pair of emerald green swim trunks. They were accented by a pale yellow diagonal stripe on one side and a matching drawstring. I walked over to where he was standing and held out the peace offering.

Ian looked wary of my kind gesture, like I was plotting more against him or up to no good.

"You should get them." I sighed before admitting, "They'll bring out the color of your eyes."

He moved away from the wall and slipped his fingers under the hanger's hook. "Thanks."

When my back was turned, I rolled my eyes at the unwelcome, stupid butterfly in my stomach and led the way to the ladies department with Reyna.

The area was a mess of empty hangers, fallen bikinis, and coverups littering the floor. Unlike the men's side, it was a barren wasteland of swimsuits. The vultures had already come and taken what they wanted, leaving the remains for us to pick through. If it hadn't been our fourth attempt of the day, I would have encouraged going to a different store. Unfortunately, the store we were in had the most options so far and we were all wearing down, hungry and tired from the early start to our day.

Reyna preferred the cute, less-revealing styles because that was what made her the most comfortable. What she picked out never failed to flatter her figure, even when her color choices were often too bright. For once, she had to settle on black as part of her deal with Wesley. The bikini stipulation wasn't technically official because I was the one who said it, not Reyna. In our minds, that was how it worked anyway.

While we searched for hers first, Wesley had his hands tucked into his back pockets, looking out of place but trying to play off casual. Ian was the opposite as he browsed the racks for the most modest swimsuit he could find for his sister. In his opinion, a wetsuit probably wouldn't be modest enough for her.

She managed to find a black one piece that would still tease and show some skin. That caused Ian to protest, but my girl cared more about what her boyfriend thought than her brother. Wesley certainly approved of it and he wasn't disappointed in the least that it wasn't a two piece.

Then it was my turn.

I used to be tall enough to stand out above the crowd, flatter than a board, and thin with about as many curves as a very straight stick. That, combined with my flexibility on the playground and the trouble I often got into, led to all the kids giving me a nickname. I blamed the girl who brought her pet ferret to show and tell one day, then the other kid who laughed and said, 'Hey, it's just like Ferra! Ferra the Ferret!'

Though I was still relatively lanky, I was no longer the tallest girl in my class and I carried myself better with a confidence I lacked in my younger years when I stuck out like a sore thumb. Dancing was a big part of where my confidence came from as I got older, along with just being sick of my peers calling me a weasel. I eventually filled out in all the right places and although I didn't have Reyna's curves, I was content enough with my own.

That was why in more recent years, two pieces were my preference for swimwear. I liked them to be tasteful yet still sexy, and as I swept through the sparse racks, I knew that would be hard to achieve but not impossible.

"Ferret," Ian whispered. He was the only person to still use that name, and I rued the day he found out about it. I ignored him so he called louder, "Ferret!"

"What?" I hissed, not bothering to turn in his direction.

"I found yours," I heard the grin in his voice.

Scoffing, I started to say, "I doubt that--"

The words died in my throat when I looked over and saw what he was holding up.

It had to be the skimpiest string bikini in the store.

With a slow, calming breath because I did not want to give him the satisfaction of seeing the blood rush to my cheeks, I tried to think of what to say to turn it back onto him.

"It's even in my color," he winked, waving the green scraps of material in my face.

Clicking my tongue, I said, "You just want to see me wearing it."

"No--"

"Ian, that's horrible," Reyna said, shaking her head in mock disappointment.

"Agreed," I crossed my arms. "You always go on about protecting your sister's innocence, but you're really just a hypocrite." I placed a hand over my heart and widened my eyes, "And what about my innocence?"

"I didn't mean it like that," Ian sputtered, embarrassment tinting his cheeks.

Wesley, knowing exactly what we were doing, took the hanger from Ian and hung it up. Then he gave him an awkward pat on the back. "Just...come stand with me and leave them alone."

Ian dejectedly lowered his head, following Wesley a few feet away from us.

Back to the task at hand, I did some mixing and matching until I found the perfect set. The top piece was white with a print of dusty pink and pale yellow flowers, while the bottom was a similar shade of pink with gold O-rings on the sides. My best friend complimented my choice and the boys remained silent as they trailed behind us to the checkout.

The food court was busy, but we were able to get a clean table that wasn't surrounded by noisy diners. While Ian guarded our table, the rest of us went to a coffee kiosk for frappes. Wesley chose an iced Americano because he's cool like that, and Ian was getting a cup of water because that was what I ordered for him. Ha.

Wesley took the drinks to our spot while the two of us walked across the court to get food for everyone. The place we all previously decided on had the best boneless chicken wings and waffle fries. Once we were seated and the mouthwatering meals distributed, we dug in like wild animals. A water fight and an afternoon of shopping worked up our appetites.

Wesley asked as he dipped a fry, "So what else do we need for the water park?"

"Sunglasses?" I suggested, giving Reyna a dry look before stabbing a piece of chicken with my fork. My gaze shifted pointedly to the borrowed pair of shades she so conveniently needed from Wesley's house. The same pair that led to her calculated seating arrangement for the ride over here. Yeah, I wasn't letting that one go just yet.

"We could all use those," she responded, flashing a grin at me. "Hey, that's a weakness of yours, isn't it? Guys in shades?"

"Yes, well, you seem to have a thing for lab coats," I said, glancing at her chemistry nerd boyfriend. "So I wouldn't be too judging, Skit."

She took a sip of her drink before quickly moving on, "We also need to get some waterproof sunscreen."

Ian scoffed at the mere mention of sunscreen. "I need to work on my tan. You people can keep your smelly lotion."

I chuckled, "I am going to laugh so hard when you end up looking like a lobster."

"I don't burn, Ferret. I glow."

"Glow like a freshly boiled lobster," Wesley mumbled before he shoved a piece of chicken into his mouth.

I was about to add to that, but an idea popped into my head that caused my mouth to snap shut. The evil plan began forming in my brilliant mind. He may not end up looking like a lobster, but he would certainly glow in the sun. Currently, I was trying not to cackle maniacally in his beautiful face.

What saved me was the song playing through the speaker above us. It was faint, but I recognized it right away.

"I love this song!" I swayed along with the music while nibbling on a waffle fry.

"You love every song," Reyna commented while her fingernail started tapping on her fork to the beat.

"That's not true, I hate any song that I can't dance to," I corrected her. "This one is my favorite for pole dancing, but it's not bad for freestyle too."

I jumped when Ian sprayed out a mouthful of water. He missed me and Reyna, but Wesley was a victim of the spit take. His face was dripping with a combination of water and saliva. Wesley pursed his lips and accepted the napkin Reyna offered to him. He wiped it off and removed his glasses to clean them, fixing a glare at Ian when they were perched back on his nose.

Ian didn't seem to care or notice as he stared at me, wide-eyed and with a gaping mouth.

"What?"

His voice cracked as he questioned, "Pole dancing?!"

It took me a moment to think about it because I didn't know why he was freaking out. When I realized his reason for reacting that way, I rolled my eyes. "Get your head out of the gutter! It's a form of dance and perfectly acceptable in today's society. It's not just for strippers anymore, dumbass."

"W-when did you--? Where did you--?"

I shrugged, "I took a class last summer."

"I wanted to join too, but apparently I'm not athletic enough for it," Reyna grumbled. It reminded of how she attempted to do it once and couldn't hold her body up. She slid, squeaking all the way down the pole like it belonged in a fire station and not a dance studio, only to end up in a heap on the floor. She never came back again after that little incident.

"But you're so young," he tried to argue with his sister, then he turned to me. "And you're like, Reyna's age."

"Yeah," I drew the word out, nodding slowly. "A few months older and eighteen soon. You say that like you aren't just a couple of years apart from us. News flash, Reyna's big brother, your little sister is all grown up."

So am I. Thank you for noticing, I thought with a pang in my chest. It wasn't a great feeling to know the guy you used to have a crush on and were still attracted to saw you as a child. I often had to defend Reyna when he treated her like a baby, but never myself because it didn't come up.

Sipping my drink, I watched him fall back in his chair as the revelation sunk into his thick skull.

The frappe didn't do much to clear the lump forming in my throat, so I looked away from Ian and smiled at Wesley. "You okay there, Wes?"

"Just great," he muttered as Reyna rubbed his arm soothingly.

"Sorry," I said because I knew Ian wouldn't apologize to him. "I didn't think mentioning that was such a big deal."

"It's not," he assured. "And you're not the one who spat all over me."

"Your shirt is all wet too," Reyna fussed over him, sending a threatening look in her brother's direction.

Wesley leaned over to whisper something in her ear. Whatever he said caused the blood to rush to her cheeks.

"Everybody ready to move on?" She asked, standing abruptly.

He smirked up at her, proud of himself for making her so flustered. We rose to our feet and Wesley collected the garbage to throw in the bin nearby.

"Earth to Ian," Reyna called when he didn't move.

I glanced down to find him staring at me. It gave me pause until I noticed the vacant look in his eyes and realized he was probably staring through me.

"Ian!" Reyna knocked the back of his head. "Let's go!"

"Maybe you didn't hit him hard enough," Wesley suggested under his breath as he returned to us and Ian still hadn't budged.

I smiled, silently agreeing with him. Yeah. Hit him harder, Skit.

Ian finally came to his senses and stood up without a word, like he wasn't whacked upside the head. He was obviously sulking as he dragged his feet, keeping his hands tucked into his pockets. The rest of us talked and laughed on our way to the next shop, but I started to feel bad and let the other two walk ahead while I fell into step with him.

Intentionally bumping into him earned me nothing but a sidelong glance. Ian looked away and I sighed, dropping my shoulders since I felt responsible for bringing him down when we were all having a good time. So I channeled my inner Reyna, who was always full of sunshine and rainbows. She was able to make even the saddest of people happy with just a few words and a smile. I was good at pep talks, but not well experienced in the field of cheering up.

I slipped my hand through his arm and squeezed to get his attention. I could feel the toned muscles in his bicep tense up when I touched him. I could have teased him about it, but chose not to do that given the circumstances. Instead I apologized for what I thought to be the true cause of his tension; the air conditioning kept the mall pretty cold, so my hands were freezing.

"Sorry, cold hands."

I started to pull away, but he tightened his arm against his side, trapping my hand in between. I gave him a questioning look, which he saw from the corner of his eye. There was a tick in his jaw before he responded, which made me wonder what was on his mind.

"It's fine," Ian muttered, loosening his grip enough for my hand to continue resting comfortably in the crook of his arm.

Unable to stop the curve of my lips, I asked, "Are you gonna live, pretty boy?"

He rolled his eyes at my term of endearment and I could see him biting back a smile. "Yes."

"She's still your little Reyndrop," I told him, using his favorite nick-name for his sister.

He exhaled a short laugh, feeling a bit better as I went on.

"And the only one she'll be stripping for is Wesley."

His fragile smile twisted into a grimace before settling into a murderous scowl.

"Easy!" My hold on his arm tightened again to prevent him from burning holes into the back of Wesley's head. Laughing despite the fact that my joke reversed the progress I made with him, I was glad just to get a reaction. "It was just a joke."

"Not funny."

"You want to know what is funny?"

He sighed, "What?"

"Your face."

Ian didn't crack in the slightest, his mood halfway back to where it was before I tried cheering him up.

I don't know how Reyna does this crap, I groaned internally.

"It's not like she took the class with me." Excluding the first time, but that didn't need mentioning. "I don't understand why you're so upset."

"It's not completely about that," he admitted.

"Then what is it?"

He kept facing ahead and sidestepped to lead me around a column I almost ran into because I wasn't looking. I didn't realize that my eyes were on him through most of our conversation. The mall was crowded, but I didn't feel even a brush of a stranger's shoulder as we walked without pause in our strides. While he may have been distracted, he still safely guided me like it was automatic for him to do and I kind of loved it.

"I'm," he hesitated to continue, "confused."

I arched a brow. "About?"

We arrived at the shop before Ian could answer me, so I stopped him at the entrance. He finally looked at me, but it was with a thoughtful expression. I found his stare unnerving and began to fidget, so I let go of his arm and took a step back to break whatever spell he was under.

After a couple of blinks, he forced a grin and responded, "Nothing. Just confused."

"Right!" I cleared my throat, then brightened my tone to say, "You're in a constant state of confusion."

"And you're in a constant state of being a Ferret."

"If you mean cute and cuddly, yes, I am." I left him behind so I could go find Reyna.

"I mean you stink!" He called out half-heartedly before I turned down the aisle where the sunscreens were located.

Reyna and Wesley were there already, choosing a brand and SPF strength. I searched the shelves for a specific type and snickered after I found it. The evil sound drew my best friend's attention and when she saw what I had in my hand, she asked me what I was plotting. They would just have to wait and see.

I was careful at the checkout so the target of my nefarious plan wouldn't see the label. I went first, putting my purchase in a small paper bag so it would remain unseen while I waited for the others. Reyna and Wesley bought the sunscreen and cheap flip-flops for everyone to wear at the water park.

All Ian bought was a pair of sunglasses.

3 | sunscreen

3 | Sunscreen

~ ☁ ☀ ☁ ~

So we wouldn't have a repeat of yesterday where we all had to cram into Ian's truck, I offered to drive everyone to the waterpark in my car. It was the best option for our hour-long trip, since it had the most space out of everyone's vehicles. Wesley met us at Reyna's house so I could pick them all up there.

I kept control of the radio with the argument 'my car, my rules' and didn't hear any complaints. It was the same excuse I gave to Ian and Wesley when I told them to ride in the backseat so Reyna could sit up front with me. There was some whining from one and irritated mutterings from the other. When I gave the ultimatum of driving there themselves, they both shut up and climbed inside.

From the rearview mirror, I could see how unhappy they were; arms crossed, looking out their own windows, and mouths turned down at the corners. I chuckled at their immaturity, drawing Ian's attention to the mirror where we made eye contact. His lips moved, forming the word 'revenge' when he saw what great pleasure I took in his suffering.

Other than that, the rest of the trip was spent singing along to the music with Reyna and the two of us ignoring the brooding boys in the back.

Once we got to the waterpark, we were able to find a parking spot near the entrance. Mornings were the best time because most of the crowds hadn't arrived yet, so we made the right decision to get there early. The four of us collected our bags from the trunk and paid to go inside the gates.

The strong chlorine combined with the smell of greasy food wafting from the vendors greeted us as we walked through. Sounds of water splashing and an occasional thrill scream could be heard ahead of us. The air was hot and a little humid, but the cold water would be the perfect remedy for it.

While the sun wasn't blazing down on us yet, we claimed our lounge chairs and pulled out the sunscreen to put on. Reyna took her cover-up off and Wesley begrudgingly peeled his shirt off.

For a nerd, he had quite the muscle definition, but I only spared him an appreciative glance and a thumbs up to Reyna. Ian came over and sat down on the chair in front of me, blocking my view of the two of them and my friend's undoubtedly flustered reaction.

"What do you want?" I asked him dryly, knowing he was up to something because of his grin.

"I'm just sitting here, Ferret," he responded in a tone of feigned innocence.

Then he reached up behind himself to grip the fabric at the back of his neck.

It was then that I knew I was going to die.

In one swift, flawless motion, he pulled his shirt off.

I was biased because I had a type and Ian Winters was the perfect example of it, but nobody could deny that he was built to perfection. My gaze lingered on his abs, not excessively defined but still a very distinct six pack. Then I moved on to his smooth chest and firm biceps, down to his forearms and back up to his face. It was impossible to hide the fact that I was checking him out, so when he smirked at me, I owned it with my head held high.

"I'm just imagining a delicious lobster," I explained, smacking my lips, "served with a side of butter and those yummy cheddar biscuits. Are you sure you don't want any sunscreen?"

He didn't say anything, only continued to smile. It turned downright smug when he slid a pair of sunglasses on, effectively hiding the mischievous twinkle in his eyes. "I'm sure."

Yep.

I was dead.

His revenge for forcing him into the backseat with Wesley was to take advantage of my weakness.

It was officially time to execute my plan.

I took off my cover-up, revealing my new two-piece swimsuit. Without regarding Ian in the slightest, I sat down and started rubbing on the regular sunscreen. When I did look over at him, I couldn't tell if he was staring. He was slack-jawed and unmoving, even with his head not aimed directly at me.

I had mixed feelings about those damn sunglasses because he looked hot in them, but it was pissing me off that I couldn't see his reaction.

Behind us, Reyna asked Wesley, "Can you put some on my back, please?"

Ian's Overprotective Mode was triggered and our flirtations were forgotten. He tried to roll to the other side of the lounge chair instead of doing the smart thing by standing up. The chair flipped over under his weight, causing him to fall onto the concrete and the chair to land on top of him. He shoved it off and stumbled to his feet.

Huffing and puffing from his harrowing battle with the chair, he pointed a threatening finger at the two of them. "There will be none of that here!"

Wesley, who already had the lotion on his hands, stared blandly at Ian like he didn't care about his girlfriend's crazy brother and was going to do it anyway. Reyna was irritated enough for both of them. She signaled for me to help her.

"Ian," I called out playfully. "Can you put some on my back? I can't reach."

Ian's head turned to me after a moment. His sunglasses had fallen off when he fought with the chair, so I could see the stunned, slow blink. Swallowing, he glanced from me to them and back again, a war—as ridiculous as the one with the lounge chair—was going on in his head.

I fluttered my lashes and gave him my best coquettish smile, "Please?"

With a very pained expression and a few forced steps closer to me, Ian reluctantly conceded came back over to me.

"I'm watching your hands, four-eyed casanova!" He warned Wesley without turning around. "I've got eyes here," he waved his hand around the back of his head. "Four of them!"

I tried not to laugh as I looked past Ian to Wesley, who scoffed and rolled his eyes.

"I saw that, Black!" Ian snapped as he placed the lounge chair back into its original upright position.

Wesley and Reyna jolted at his declaration. I was surprised Ian didn't feel the stabbing sensation from the daggers their glares were throwing his way. I turned to face the pool and moved forward to make room for Ian to sit behind me. Then I felt the chair dip a little as he sat down.

"Eyes on the side of my head too," he announced while they were probably ignoring him. "I'm like a jumping spider. A 360 view of my prey at all times!"

"Shut up, Ian." I tossed the lotion over my shoulder to him. "They're not gonna do anything with children around."

I smirked when he choked on his own spit.

When he recovered, he muttered closely to my ear, "Careful, Ferret. I might miss a couple of spots."

The way his breath tickled that sensitive area below my ear was ruined by the irritated pout I could hear in his voice. He also sounded distracted, like he was still watching them and not focusing on me.

With a frustrated sigh, I swept my hair up and twisted it into a bun so sunscreen wouldn't get in it. Straightening my posture, I waited for him to put the lotion on. It seemed to take him a minute or two, but that may have been my own impatience to get to the next phase of my plan.

I never liked the feel of sunscreen, but it was better than the alternative of burning. The worst part of it was the initial application, but once it was all rubbed in, I didn't mind it so much.

Ian changed my opinion as soon as his hand glided down my spine.

He used both hands to spread the lotion out from the center, starting at the base of my neck to my shoulders and working his way down. The pressure of his palms and the circular motions he used made it feel like a massage. My eyelids fell shut at the soothing sensation as he moved his hands lower, slowly making his way to the small of my back.

Because I danced so often, pain in my lower back would sometimes flare up if I overworked myself. So when he pressed his palms there and kneaded the muscles, an involuntary moan escaped from my throat.

It was barely audible, but he must have heard it because his hands ceased all movement, stopping on my hips. My eyes shot open and I fought the urge to bury my head in my hands or flat out run away.

It wasn't a big deal, right? I asked myself. There was no reason other than it just felt good, but he must have known that it was not in that way. Just yesterday he practically called me a kid, so his mind wouldn't go straight to the gutters over a tiny sound. But what if his mind did and I just humiliated myself?

Ian cleared his throat.

No! It was his fault. I asked for sunscreen, not a massage.

His hands resumed the motion, but he slid them up higher and stayed far away from my lower back.

"This sunscreen is kind of nice. It smells good," Ian commented. His voice was thick, but he was trying his best to move on.

He was lucky that he didn't bring attention to it, because I would have knocked him out in hopes that he would wake up with short term memory loss.

I exhaled the breath I was holding and relaxed as I went on with my plan. "Are you sure you don't want to put some on?"

He was done with my back, but I didn't want to face him yet.

"Come on," I pushed. "You don't really want to deal with a sunburn, do you? The burning, the itching, the peeling skin..." I shuddered for effect.

"Alright, alright," he sighed. "I'll try some."

I thought I succeeded in not showing my enthusiasm, but I still stood up too quickly. "Perfect! I'll do your back as thanks for doing mine."

I stepped around Ian, nudging him to scoot forward so I could sit down behind him. I silently reached into my bag beside the chair and pulled out the other sunscreen.

I hummed a happy tune while I squeezed some of it into my palm and Ian held his hand out for some to do his chest and arms. I wiped it onto his from mine so he wouldn't see the different bottle. I was already concerned he would see the difference in the lotion or with the smell of it. I only hoped that he wouldn't notice until after he put it on.

By then it would be too late.

When I started to rub the lotion into his back, I sucked my lips into my mouth so I wouldn't laugh out loud. My face had to be turning red at the effort I put in to stay quiet, but I had to wait for him to see it.

His skin shimmered like Edward Cullen on a hot summer day.

"Ferra," I heard him growl.

The idiot didn't even realize it until he was done with his chest and halfway down one of his arms. By then, I was finished with his back.

The laughter burst out of me and I couldn't stop. I collapsed back against the lounge chair, holding my side because it hurt from the cackling. My head was pounding from the lack of oxygen and I had a bad case of hiccups after the hysterics ended, but it was so very worth it.

Reyna's reaction was similar to mine. Even Wesley chuckled when he saw what I did to Ian.

"Is this going to come off?" The sparkly vampire asked me.

"Most of it will be gone by the end of the day," I grinned, patting his shoulder. "It's not that bad."

Once the lotion was rubbed in completely, it left a gold shimmer on his skin that didn't look all that awful.

Unfortunately.

"If only you were paler," I sighed. "With sharper teeth and better reflexes."

"If I were a vampire, I'd bite you first," he muttered as he scrubbed his arms with a towel.

I was only brave enough to say the words I was thinking of because he wasn't facing me.

"You don't have to be a vampire to nibble on my neck."

Then I left him there without looking back. Wrapping my arm around Reyna's shoulder, I told Wesley to grab her hand or fall behind as we went on to the first water slide.

4 | Lemonade

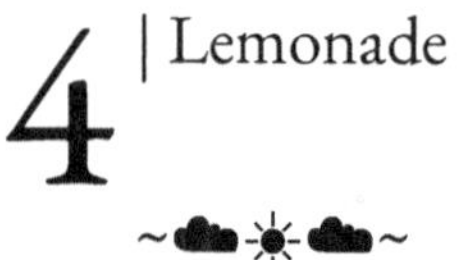

"Look," I began as I rested my hand on my hip and glanced at the guy's nametag, "Richard. All my friend here wants is a Skittle milkshake. Is that so complicated?"

"Seriously," Reyna scowled as she slammed a red packet on the counter. "I'm even supplying my own Skittles. All you have to do is throw it in the blender with vanilla ice cream and press a button."

"Uh," he blinked. Then he repeated for the third time, "It's not on the menu though."

"Come on, Skit," I gave him a disapproving shake of my head as I turned my friend away. "Let's leave Dick alone and go over there. They have waffle cones, which are better than milkshakes anyway."

"Nah," she declined, tearing open her packet of candy while we walked. "How about we get some fresh lemonade for us and the boys?"

By some miracle, Ian and Wesley bonded over The Drip Drop. They enjoyed it so much that they got back in line to go down the slide a second time.

I personally didn't like being shut in a box and having the floor fall out from under me. I screamed the whole way down until I hit the water and swore I would not be doing it again. Since we spent the past two hours in the water, Reyna and I left them alone because we were ready for a break.

The park had gotten significantly more busy, so the line for the lemonade was long. While we waited, we discussed which water slide was the best. Then we got on the subject of our game of Marco Polo.

"I still can't believe that guy didn't kick Ian's ass," Reyna said.

Reyna responded 'Polo' to her brother's 'Marco' after he caught Wesley and me. Ian thought he was close enough to her voice when he lunged forward, but he landed on a guy who had to be an aspiring body builder. He was twice the size of Ian with thrice the muscles. He had the impeccable timing of swimming by at just the right moment.

The worst part about it was Ian felt up the guys arms in confusion before opening his eyes and seeing what—or rather whom—he caught.

"Y-you're not my sister," was what he said.

The guy looked ready to pummel Ian and turn the water red with his blood, but a little girl called for her dad. His angry expression softened at the sound of her voice, so he shoved Ian away and swam over to his daughter in the shallow end.

"Honestly," I told Reyna as we drew closer to the lemonade, "I think Ian's hug with death was the highlight of my day."

"Even over the shimmering sunscreen?"

"It didn't last long enough," I frowned. "Shouldn't have bought the cheap brand."

"No, I meant putting it on him."

I was used to denying or hiding whatever residual feelings I had from crushing on him, so my response was a reflex when I said, "Don't be gross."

"I wasn't," she chuckled, stepping forward as the line moved up. "I'm just making sure that you know I support you."

"Yeah. I got that, Skit. You're like a brass band in a library."

With a laugh, she apologized, "I'm sorry, Fere. I'll try to show my support more discreetly from now on."

"You can start with discreetly supporting my wallet by paying for the lemonade," I told her and ordered four cups.

While she was paying for them, I stepped off to the side with a satisfied smirk.

"Ferra!"

I turned in the direction where my name was called, surprise crossing my features at who I saw standing there.

"Noelle!"

"Who?" Reyna asked, appearing beside me and struggling to balance the four lidded cups.

I took two from her and sipped one of them while Noelle introduced herself to my friend. She owned a dance studio in our city. I participated in some of her classes since I was a preteen up to just last summer and I signed up for more later this season too. She was even going to write a letter of recommendation for my college admissions.

"Oh! You're the one who taught her how to pole-dance!"

Noelle laughed, "No, but I did tell Ferra about it and suggested a class to check out. She excels in almost every style of dance." She shook her head, "I swear this girl is going to put me out of business when she gets older."

"I will not," I bristled.

"Then buy my studio from me so I can properly retire."

Noelle retired from professional dancing, but her studio was where she found true happiness. She was a role model to me, but I could only hope to have my own studio someday and be as accomplished as her.

I shook my head, "You're too young to put your dancing shoes away."

She playfully rolled her eyes.

Reyna politely excused herself, "I think I see my boyfriend, so I'll leave you guys to talk dance. It was nice to meet you!"

"It was nice to meet you too." As soon as Reyna was gone, Noelle spoke again. "I'm glad I ran into you, Ferra."

"I know, I know," I waved my hand. "It's always a pleasure to see your favorite prodigy."

Noelle crossed her arms, raising a sculpted brow at my arrogance. "No, actually. I need a favor, if you're up to the task. I've been trying to think of who to ask and it just occurred to me that you would be perfect for it."

"For what?" I asked her with peaked interest.

"My husband and I are taking our daughter and her friends on a weekend trip," she started.

"Well, you're going to have your hands full," I commented, thinking of my little sister. It was a nightmare when she had friends over, so I often spent my time at Reyna's house. I rarely let my bestie come over to mine for that very reason. That, and Meg monopolized Reyna's time so much that I imagined her wearing a little top hat and twisting a mustache below her button nose.

"I know," she said, looking tired at the mere thought of it. "Anyway, we're leaving on Friday, but I have a class scheduled for that afternoon. I've just hired a new assistant, but I can't leave him to teach a class right after he's started working there. Is there any chance you would be willing to do it?"

"I don't know," I hesitated.

"It's a senior tango class, so just the basics. Alex will be there to help you with whatever you need too."

I gave her a skeptical look. I didn't feel confident in my ability to teach a class just yet. Teaching was leaps and bounds from learning. Then again, I did have to start somewhere and now was as good a time as any.

"Everyone in the class is very laid back. They'll adore you and possibly pinch your cheeks," she laughed lightly in a poor attempt to convince me.

It was having the opposite effect, but I nodded anyway. "I'll do it."

"Mom!" Came the impatient screech of her twelve year old daughter.

"I just love that sound," Noelle stated sarcastically and sighed. "I'll call you on Monday with the details."

We both said goodbye and went our separate ways. I couldn't stop smiling on the short trip back to the lounge area. I drank more of my lemonade and put the two cups down on the pavement beside me. Then I leaned back on my chair with a satisfied sigh and closed my eyes.

The sun was pleasantly warm with the heat soaking into my skin, giving me pleasant tingles all over. Reyna and Wesley were both laying on their chairs too, talking about what he and Ian got up to while we were apart. I relaxed while listening to the conversation.

"How many times did you guys do that water slide?"

"Four," Wesley answered. "By the fourth drop, the adrenaline rush started wearing off and I got bored with it."

Bored...he got bored of falling almost thirty feet into a pool?!

"Did you have fun though?" She chuckled, "Before the epinephrine wore off?"

"Yes, but I enjoyed the ones you and I did together more." His voice lowered in a way that I almost didn't hear him say, "I prefer the rush I get from being that close to you."

I cracked an eye open when it got very quiet, only to discover them kissing. I lifted a brow when they didn't stop and cleared my throat. I quickly shut my eyes again when they broke out of their liplock to look at me. I was opposed to interrupting them, but they risked getting kicked out with that kind of PDA. I fought a smile when they tried to casually continue their conversation.

"Oh! We should do the Swirl Whirl again before we leave," Reyna chirped, sounding a little too breathless.

"We could go now," Wesley offered in a deeper, slightly hoarse tone.

I smirked, Need some of that cold water washing over you, Black?

"That's a good idea." Then, as if it was just dawning on her, she said, "Wait a minute. Where's Ian?"

"He got caught by two girls on our way over. From what I gathered, he dated one of them in the past. He's right there."

Curiosity getting the best of me, I peeked my eyes open again to see where Wesley was pointing. Ian's back still had some shimmer to it, making his identity unmistakable. The girls talking to him—or rather giggling—wore string bikinis unfit for a family-friendly water park. And the way they were looking at him like hyenas who just found their next meal made me shudder for him. Ian kept glancing back at us, his tight-lipped smile dropping as he mouthed something.

"What is he doing?" Reyna asked, squinting to try to see better.

I sat up, watching more closely with her as we waited for him to look back at us again. Meanwhile, his hands were flailing behind his back as if he were signaling to us for...

"'Help?'" Reyna read his lips and laughed. "He wants us to help him?"

Wesley chimed in, "He didn't seem to want me to leave him alone with them."

"What do you think, Ferra?" Reyna looked at me, her eyes twinkling with humor, "Should we help him or leave him to suffer?"

Without voicing an answer, my body started moving of its own accord. I stood up, adjusted my swimsuit and then fixed my hair. Thank goodness it was still wet and not frizzy dry. Taking a deep breath, I straightened my shoulders and pushed my chest out before approaching the three of them. I had to play the part of a girlfriend staking her claim. That was the only way to get the hungry hyenas to back off. Yeah. I could do it.

As I got closer, I could hear one of the girls say, "It's a shame that you took a gap year before college. You missed out on all of the good parties."

Ian chuckled tensely and scratched the back of his neck, "Sorry, girls."

After more of their obnoxious giggling, the one who did most of the talking reached out to stroke his arm. "That's okay. We can show you around campus when you join us. You would really like my dorm room."

Why? He'd only be interested if there were a cabinet of snacks and a bean bag chair. I quickened my pace anyway.

"I don't think—"

I cut Ian off from only a few steps away with a shrill, "Excuse me!"

The girl who had been groping him dropped her arm and gave me a dirty look.

I was known for being dramatic, so if I had to save his ass, then I was going to put on one hell of a show doing it.

"Care to tell me why you had your hands all over my boyfriend?"

"Boyfriend?" She glanced disbelievingly between the two of us.

She was waiting for Ian to confirm or deny it, but he did neither by just standing there dumbfounded, heavy on the dumb. It wasn't going to work if he didn't play along.

"Yes, boyfriend. Something you clearly don't have," I said, sizing her up the same way she did to me.

Ian's eyes widened a fraction as our eyes met, drawn out of his stupor. I smiled as I wrapped my arms around his waist, urging him to respond. His hand slid around to rest on my hip as he finally took the hint and jerked me closer. My palm flew to his chest for balance when I stumbled forward, but I left it there for the act.

"Baby," I purred in a sultry tone that surprised the both of us. I didn't think he noticed his own sharp intake of breath or his hand flex on my hip, but I did and I relished in it. "Make them go away so I don't have to do it myself. I'd much rather spend my energy on..."

I leaned into him and whispered his ear.

To the two girls, I was saying what explicit things I wanted to do with him.

In reality, I whispered, "...throwing you off a cliff into the shallow end of a pool."

The smile that formed on Ian's lips was genuine and he bit his lip so he wouldn't outright laugh, which only added to the girls' imaginations running wild.

He tightened his hold, pulling me flush up against his side. I hoped my smile didn't falter at the intimate contact of my body pressed against his, all while trying not to think about the possibility of Ian feeling how fast my heart was racing out of my chest.

The other girl, who had been the quiet, loyal minion to her friend, backed away a few steps before turning around and walking away.

"If it wasn't already obvious, I'm not interested," Ian said to the one who hadn't left yet, his polite tone a contradiction to his harsh words. If only he had said that to them sooner, but he was either a coward or too nice.

"You're not that much of catch anyway, Ian. Just good eye candy." She flipped her hair and turned to follow her retreating minion. Then she called over shoulder, "She can have you."

When they were out of sight, I shoved Ian away from me. I muttered about the girl, "Better to be eye candy than bitch candy." Then to Ian, I said, "Don't listen to her."

He shrugged, "I'm not. I know I'm a great catch and eye candy."

I snorted, but didn't say anything to the contrary. I was too distracted by the warm sensation where his hand was a minute ago. The feeling of his thumb idly rubbing back and forth on my bare skin lingered even with the distance between us.

"Thanks for saving me, Ferret." Ian grinned, tilting his head slightly. He had one eye shut from the glare of the sun like he was winking.

I turned my head away from him, wrinkling my nose at the nickname.

He chuckled and threw his arm around me. "Come on. Let's go make sure those two are keeping it PG."

5 | Cooler

Camping was something Reyna and I did every summer for the past eight years. It was a tradition for our families to pack up for a five hour drive and a few nights in nature. I wasn't a super outdoorsy person, but I did like camping as long as I had bug spray and I always had fun with my best friend.

We were fortunate that our families got along so well too. My mom and Reyna's mom were like older, more chill versions of the two of us. Although they usually spend the trip reading trashy romance novels together and we weren't into that phase yet.

Meanwhile, my little sister was forced to spend time with our dad because he rarely got quality time with her. Megan was much more girly than tomboy-and speaking of phases, she was at that age where she wanted to be a princess-but our dad insisted on teaching her everything about wilderness survival. Just in case she ever gets lost in the woods for a week, because the odds of that happening were...to be honest, not very likely.

He convinced her that she could still be a princess and know how to save herself. Then she took her own take on that by saying that she would save her prince instead of waiting for him to come to her. While he didn't like the sound of that, he was desperate for some company after his attempts to teach me and Reyna simultaneously, then Ian until my dad got tired of all three of us.

Regarding Ian, he was tag-along because he felt responsible for us. In reality, he just didn't have anyone to hang out with on his own. He used to annoy his sister and I pretended to feel the same for her benefit, but I liked his company since I was crushing on him so hard at the time. Now we both found him equally annoying and pleasant to be around.

I hoped our tradition would continue well after high school and college. I imagined everyone meeting up for it every year no matter where we were in our lives. None of us would ever miss a single minute of our families' camping trip.

Yet I was going to miss most of the first day.

"My parents reminded me that the camping trip was moved up because of my dad's work schedule. Since I completely forgot that important detail, I accepted an offer to fill in for a dance class tomorrow," I recounted to Reyna on speakerphone.

We were both packing our bags for the next few days and I was in the process of picking out what clothes I wanted to wear.

"So what are you going to do?" Reyna asked, her voice sounding distant like she had her head in her closet too.

"You guys are leaving in the morning as planned, and I'm going to join you right after the class is over. I won't miss much and I'll be there in plenty of time for s'mores." I folded my shirts and put them on top of the shorts and pants I stuffed into the bottom of my bag.

"Are your parents okay with you driving that far alone? Not to mention the short hike to the campsite in the dark," she said, not lowering her voice when she moved closer to the phone. She was the type to think she has to talk louder just because she was on speaker.

I didn't say anything about it, but turned the volume down on my phone so my ears weren't tweaking. "Well," I grimaced, "they kind of have to be since I made a commitment to do the class. And I hope I don't sound selfish in saying that I really want to do it."

"You don't, Fere," Reyna assured me. "I think it's a great opportunity for you."

"Thanks, Skit." I smiled at how supportive she was of my dancing.

Whenever I tried to show off my dance skills on the playground when we were little, the other kids laughed instead of being impressed like I hoped they would be. Reyna was the one who clapped and cheered me on. We became the best of friends when I shared a bag of Skittles with her that my mom packed with my lunch. Her eyes still lit up the same way they did back then whenever she was given her favorite candy.

"At the same time," I began, collapsing onto my bed after putting my pajamas into the bag and zipping it up. "I hate missing out on some of our camp adventures."

She laughed. "Please, you're getting out of pitching the tents and firewood hunting." Then she had a eureka moment and my volume at its lowest setting couldn't handle her shout, "Hey! Maybe I should stay with you!"

"Stay with who?"

If I were a puppy, my ears would have perked at the sound of Ian's voice.

"Ferra. She's meeting us at the campsite later because she has a dance class to teach," Reyna announced proudly.

"Ah," I could picture him crossing his arms and leaning in her doorway. "So you're trying to get out of helping us set up by staying with her. I don't think so, Reyns. It's part of the experience!"

I teased, "And just think of what Ian and my dad will do to Wesley if you're not there to protect him."

"Ferret has a good point. I'm thinking some sort of initiation is in order..."

"Fine! No getting out of it," Reyna conceded.

I was curious about what evil plan Ian would have devised, so it was a shame she gave in that quickly.

"Great teamwork, Ferret!"

"I didn't do it for you, dummy. I did it on behalf of Team Reyley. That doesn't mean you don't get to give Wes an initiation, but I do insist you wait for me-"

Reyna cut me off, "Ferra!"

"So I can make sure it doesn't get out of hand!" I finished in a defensive tone. Then more sheepishly, I added, "I can also take pictures."

Ian's approving laughter was muffled after a few seconds by Reyna's bedroom door slamming in his face. I chuckled as I listened to them exchanging shouts. He was upset about being excluded from the conversation and she was upset about his existence. She came back over to the phone a few minutes later after their mom yelled at them to shut up.

"Now that he's gone, I wanted to ask you something," she hesitated. "Are you really okay with Wes and his mom coming with us?"

"Of course I am. Our moms are already practically BFFs with his mom and you know I'm cool with Wesley."

Reyna heaved a sigh of relief. She must have been worried about it for awhile. "Thanks, Fere."

I smiled again, "Welcome, Skit."

As soon as we got off the phone, Megan barged into my room without knocking.

"Ferra, Daddy wants me to wear khaki pants with a bunch of pockets. They're ugly!" She whined and poked her bottom lip out. "Please help me pack so I don't have to wear ugly clothes like him."

I laughed, not falling for her pout like so many others do. "First of all, how do you even know what 'khaki' means?"

"He told me when he buyed them."

"Bought," I corrected her.

"That's what I said!"

I rolled my eyes.

"Anyway! They came from where the boys' clothes are, not the girls' clothes."

"So? I wear boy clothes sometimes," I admitted with a shrug. "A lot of girls do."

My personal favorite was one of Ian's hoodies whenever he let me and Reyna borrow them. They were like a snuggly blanket that could hug. Not to mention the lingering smell of his body wash and fabric softener on the clean material. I also wore some oversized shirts for dance practice and often slept in them too. I failed to mention to her that I wouldn't wear anything like that out in public because, like her, it just wasn't my style.

"Not me," she puffed her cheeks and crossed her arms.

"Fine, whatever," I sighed. "Why can't mom help you?"

"Because she said..." she took a second to remember, "she's getting food peppered for the trip."

"Prepared?"

"That's what I said!" She barked again, as if she was annoyed at me for mishearing her. We both knew she didn't say that, but it wasn't worth the effort of arguing with a six-year-old. "So will you help me? Please?"

My little sister wasn't going to leave me alone until I did exactly what she wanted, so I got up and followed Megan to her room. Our dad had her pink bag halfway full, humming a tune while he folded the khaki pants. I understood why she was protesting after seeing the pants myself. He smiled when Meg came into the room, but his lips fell into a frown when he saw me. With a dejected sigh, he tossed the pants on the twin bed.

"I get it. The princess doesn't want to be a pauper for a few days, just to make her old man happy."

Meg and I shared a look and a cringe. Neither of us were falling for his act, so I stepped in to handle it. I took my dad's hand, patting the back of it in consolation.

"Dad, we love you. And we want you to be happy..." I smiled. "But even I wouldn't be caught dead in those things."

"That's a shame, Ferra dear." He took my hand in both of his, returning the comforting action as his sad expression turned smug. "Because I bought a pair of pants for you too."

I blinked a few times. "What?"

"Yep," he crossed his arms. "I'm also using my authority as your father to order the both of you to wear them on the trip." He started to leave, but stopped at the door to say, "If it makes you two feel better, you will always be my princesses."

Meg and I watched him go, stunned and angry as we gaped at his retreating back. I technically didn't have to listen to him and Meg didn't either, because he wouldn't be upset or ground us over such a miniscule disobedience to a petty order. Though instead of just leaving the pants behind, I felt an ounce of revenge needed to be served.

"If we're the princesses, he's the evil bitch who cursed us," Meg muttered and hopped onto her bed.

I gaped at the language she used and corrected quickly, "Witch, Megan! He's a witch."

"That's what I said!"

"Well, I say we break the curse," I grinned at her, disregarding her blatant cussing in favor of some sister bonding.

The look on our dad's face would be priceless.

After Megan went to sleep, I stayed up late to finish what we started together. So I was half-asleep in the morning when they woke me up to say goodbye. I didn't bother changing out of my night shirt since I had every intention of going back to sleep after they left, so I put my robe on over it and stepped into my slippers. I trudged out into the living room, yawning and scratching my bed head while my parents bustled around.

My mom was alternating between guzzling her coffee and filling two large coolers. My dad was running in and out of the house to load up the SUV.

She was relieved to see me, "Ferra, can you check on your sister and see if she's ready to go?"

I nodded lazily, but before I could do it, Meg came running out on her own. She flew past me to our mom and twirled around.

"Mommy, look what I did," she smiled proudly. I cleared my throat and Meg added without even glancing at me, "And Ferra helped."

Brat, I thought with a sleepy scowl.

Gone were the hideous khaki pants, replaced with what could only be called a Megan Chandler Original. I told her it would be too much, but she insisted on adding the pink tulle. The pants were cut into shorts and bedazzled with rhinestones and glitter. Then, as per her orders, a layer of hot pink tulle covered all the work I did for her.

There was nothing practical about what she was wearing because the netting would be gone as soon as it snagged on a branch. Fortunately, I wouldn't be there to hear her whining about it. She would get over it after seeing the bling it was hiding from the sunlight.

"You look beautiful, Meg," our mom said before throwing me a withering look.

I mouthed, "What?!"

Her response was a roll of her eyes as she took a long sip of coffee. I didn't know how my dad could survive such attitude from the three of us without going crazy.

"What did you do?!"

He was the Drama King after all, so it balanced out.

"I made it better, daddy," Meg sniffed with her chin up. "I would rather wear a garbage bag than those pants. At least it would be shiny!"

He simply sighed and pinched the bridge of his nose.

Mom chimed in with a mutter, "This is what happens when I don't do the packing. You've all got screws loose."

Dad either didn't hear her or ignored her when he turned his disappointed gaze to me. "Do I want to know what you did with yours?"

I sucked in my lips and shook my head. They weren't nearly as gaudy as Megan's, but they were shorter and had their own fair share of studs and gems. Mine weren't technically practical either, but we were making a statement and I was going to stand with my little sister on it. Plus they looked really good on me after I was finished with them. All the modifications I made to my dance costumes over the years had paid off well.

"Honey," dad gave mom a look of despair, "can we have a son?"

Her answer was an immediate and firm, "No."

"You can have two son-in-laws, daddy!"

He stared down at his youngest daughter for a minute, his features hardening as he thought about what she said. I could see the horror in his eyes as his mind reeled with the possibilities of grooms and marriage. He blinked a few times and smiled tightly, "I was only kidding. I love my two beautiful daughters and I don't need sons of any kind."

Meg returned his smile brightly.

He was just played by a six-year-old.

No one was immune to her manipulative charms, except me and our mom. Even Reyna fell prey to my little sister and was beyond saving. I didn't know if I should applaud or frown upon her ways.

As they gathered the last of the camping essentials, I followed them out to the driveway. They would be going to the Winters' residence to meet up with them, Wesley, and his mom. Then after sorting out carpooling arrangements, they would all be on their way without me. It bummed me out to miss the ride, but I looked forward to joining them soon.

"Be careful," my dad looked pointedly at me from the driver's seat.

"I will."

"You know there's no reception out there, so you won't be able to contact us," my mom warned. "If it's dark by the time you get there, sleep in your car and come to us in the morning. Do not walk through the woods at night. Got it?"

I cocked my hip and raised a brow at her. We had been to the same area for years, so I knew exactly where it was and how to get there. When her expression dared me not to answer correctly without talking back, I said, "Fine. I'll wait. That won't be a problem anyway since I should be there before it gets dark."

My mom bit her bottom lip, "I don't know if this is such a good idea."

I could tell that my dad was about to agree and shut it all down, so I started to back away quickly.

"It'll be fine! I promise! You have to let me be a responsible adult and keep my commitment. I love you guys! See you soon! Bye!" I rushed out and spun on my heels.

I walked at a hurried pace to the door and shut it before they could say anything else. Leaning against the door, I took a breath before glancing out of the window. A smile tugged the corners of my mouth up as I watched them reverse out onto the street. Stretching my arms above my head, I climbed the steps to my bedroom.

Another hour of sleep was calling to me and it would be rude not to answer.

6 | Ice Cream Sandwich

One of the many perks of being home alone was waking up peacefully. No little sister or best friend jumping on your bed. No parents waking you ten minutes before your alarm goes off, causing you to lose that precious last bit of sleep.

It was just me, my pillow and blankets, and my alarm set to play a pleasant melody in one hour.

So upon hearing a male voice before that hour was up and feeling a hand on my arm, I did what any half-asleep person would do if they were home alone.

I screamed and blindly punched in the direction of the voice.

My fist made contact and I heard a grunt of pain. Hissing through my teeth at the throbbing ache in my knuckles, I shot up to better defend myself.

"What the hell was that for, Ferret?!"

I screamed back at him, "What the hell are you doing here, Ian?!"

I was wide awake after that scare and my heart beating out of my chest. The initial fear was gone, quickly replaced with an anger that simmered down to annoyance when I saw his hand cupped over his nose.

His voice was muffled as he said, "I think you broke it."

"I did not hit you that hard," I huffed, getting out of bed and stepping over to him. "Let me see."

Ian's gaze followed my movements, dropping down from my night shirt to my bare legs before darting away. I pulled his hand away so I could see the damage I caused, if there was any at all. His nose was a bit redder than the tint creeping up his cheeks.

"Did I just hit your nose? Or the surrounding area too?"

He scoffed, refusing to meet my eyes when I gave him a teasing grin. Though he couldn't seem to resist another glance at my legs.

"You could've warned me that you weren't decent under the blankets," he muttered. "Or stayed in bed."

"Your fault for exaggerating about your nose," I shrugged. "I had to make sure it wasn't broken. Besides, I am far better than decent so I don't know why you're complaining."

I would have flipped my hair, but the nest of a bun on top of my head wouldn't allow it. I honestly didn't care about my appearance in front of him because he had seen me in more unattractive clothing than what I was wearing.

Judging by his reaction and wandering eyes, an oversized shirt that rested mid-thigh didn't make that list. So I had no reason to be embarrassed and instead basked in the glory of making Ian Winters uncomfortable.

I poked the tip of his sore nose, making him flinch and drawing his attention away from the wall. And the ceiling. And the floor.

"So are you going to tell me why you're here?" I backed up to my bed and sat down on the edge of it, making a point of crossing one leg over the other.

He was seemingly unaffected by my action as he answered, "I am your chauffeur today."

My cocky expression collapsed. "What?"

"Your parents were worried about you making the trip alone, so they asked me to stay behind with you."

Humiliation and anger warred within me until they joined forces, causing an outburst that I regretted as soon as the words left my mouth.

"I don't need a babysitter," I scowled.

He held his hands out in surrender and said his favorite line to use whenever I was mad at him, "Don't get feral on me, Ferret."

I crossed my arms and glared at him and he had the nerve to chuckle. I wasn't doing myself any favors, but I was offended and embarrassed that my parents did that, and to Ian of all people!

"Look, I wouldn't like to make the drive by myself because it would be lonely and boring. So..." he exhaled and shoved his hands into his back pockets, hesitating as if he had a big confession to make. "So I offered to stay behind because I didn't want you to have to do it alone."

"Oh," was all I could say. It was my turn to blush, but it mostly had to do with my behavior. If only he had said that first, instead of leading me to believe it was all my parents' doing. "I, um, need to get ready to go. I can't be late for the class."

"Okay," he sounded eager to move on and get out of my room. "I'll be waiting downstairs. Take your time."

I watched him hurry out and stayed where I was for a few minutes after he left. I could never tell if his care was brotherly or something else, because I always had a habit of reading too much into the behavior and actions of others. Maybe I was doing that to him too.

Shaking my head, I jumped to my feet and got dressed.

There was no room in my mind to overthink when it was time to dance.

"You know, a bag of frozen peas would have been better," I commented as we walked into the empty dance studio.

Ian insisted on driving me there in his truck. I offered to meet up afterwards, but he asked if he could stick around since he had nothing to do. With a healthy dose of sarcasm, I told him what an honor it was to be his cure for boredom.

He was allowed to stay, but with the stipulation that he had to participate in the lesson. The guy couldn't dance to save his life, so he could benefit from learning a few moves.

He agreed to my terms without knowing who his fellow students would be, or to be more precise, their age range.

Ian sat down on one of the chairs lining the far wall, while holding a packaged ice cream sandwich against his nose.

"I know," he said as he readjusted the frozen treat to the other side, "but I can't eat those when I'm done and a convenience store doesn't carry vegetables."

I smiled, "That's true. I suppose frozen vegetables aren't very convenient."

"Exactly," he grinned and peeled off the wrapper to enjoy the melting ice cream.

When I moved over to the stereo, I found a note from Noelle. She informed me that the music was all set up for the lesson with a 'Good luck!!!' at the bottom of the page. Some nerves were starting to set in, but there was just as much excitement too.

I was going to start warming up, but the heavy door squeaking open stopped me mid-stretch. My heart leaped to my throat at the sound of my first student arriving. The jittery feelings wouldn't stop until the actual dancing began, so I took a breath and shook my hands out before turning around with a welcoming smile.

Instead of seeing a senior person ready to learn how to tango, I saw the broad back of a very fit man in very tight clothing. He kicked the door stopper down then faced me with a blinding smile.

I wasn't one for scruff, but the five-o'clock shadow over his sculpted jaw worked wonders for him and complimented the warm undertones of his flawless skin. His eyes were such a dark brown that they almost looked purple and they were twinkling at me.

"You must be Ferra," he spoke with a rich accent as he took my hand and kissed the back of it. "I will be your assistant today."

"You're Alex?" My voice came out a little too breathy than I intended. I barely even registered Ian's sudden presence beside me.

"My full name is Alejandro," he explained, "but Alex is easier on the tongue."

I couldn't refrain a small giggle when he smiled at me.

"That's like the Lady Gaga song, right?" Ian asked, nudging me aside to shake Alex's hand. "How does it go? 'She's not your babe.' Something like that..."

I blinked out of my stupor and scowled at Ian.

"Please forgive Rudolph the Red-Nosed dipshit over here," I referred to his sore nose and jammed my elbow into his ribs as I spoke to Alex. "He's going to be sitting in, if that's alright?"

"Of course your boyfriend can stay! Rudolph is a very," Alex paused as if to think of the right word to use, "interesting name."

"My name is Ian," he corrected with a frown.

I waited two beats to see if he was going to correct the other misunderstanding. When he didn't, I added, "He's also not my boyfriend. Ian is more like a guard dog."

"I see," Alex nodded slowly, though he seemed to be a little confused. "Ah! A bodyguard for the beautiful lady, yes?"

I would have melted like that ice cream sandwich if Ian's glare wasn't already scolding me. It may have been wrong to call him a guard dog, but he was certainly acting like one and he had no right to do so.

Our conversation was cut short when a group of older people shuffled into the room, chatting and laughing boisterously. More followed as they trickled in for the dance lesson and I felt my stomach drop. I recognized some of the faces, but most of them were new to me.

I shoved Ian in their direction and a few of the ladies eyed him curiously as he took his place beside them. One woman got a little handsy as she stroked his bicep and I ignored his look that said, 'What have you gotten me into, Ferret?'

"Hello," my voice was shaky, but it couldn't rival my hands. "My name is Ferra and I'm filling in for Noelle today. I'm sure you've all had the privilege of meeting Alex already."

With a charming smile directed at them, he inclined his head as a greeting.

"Alex, would you be so kind as to tell them what we're going to be learning this afternoon?"

I was used to the spotlight when it came to dancing, even though I still got nervous before a performance. Speaking while in the spotlight was completely different and I had yet to master it. I rubbed my sweaty palms on my leggings and moved aside for Alex to explain and show them the basic tango steps.

"I thought this was supposed to be a sexy dance," complained the woman who had her hand on Ian's arm.

The men and women chuckled, most of them nodding their heads in agreement. Alex and I shared a look and laughed at their enthusiasm and expectations. Noelle was right when she said they were pretty chill, so I could feel my nerves beginning to settle.

"I assure you that it can be," Alex assured her in a playfully defensive tone. "Would you like us to demonstrate?"

He pressed play on the stereo, starting a slow song that had the perfect rhythm and snappy notes for a tango. Alex's hands slid boldly around my waist and he twirled me to face him.

"Is this okay?" He asked softly so they couldn't hear. "You looked nervous so I thought a bit of dancing would help."

"Let's do this," I told him as I put my hand in his and the other rested on his arm. I smiled at the handsome kindred spirit in front of me, already feeling the music smothering my nerves into nonexistence.

Tango was all about passion. It could be sensual, angry, full of love, or any combination of the three. It was an artform. The man, a statue for the woman to dance around. Then a shift to the woman being an instrument for the man to worship. And in between, lovers fighting for dominance over the other and neither knowing who would be victorious until the end of the song.

I was rusty with the more intricate moves, but Alex made it easy to follow his lead and each stroke of his hands instilled a confidence in my limbs that would have otherwise been lost with every fumble. The tango we did was intermediate compared to the beginner steps we would be teaching, but they wanted a show and we gave one to them.

The music guided us, displaying a sensual passion on the surface, but beneath that I was only dancing with an attractive stranger. All the emotion I felt was superficial, due to fade after the dance was over.

Ian crossed my mind once as I felt his gaze on me, but when I missed a step, I pushed him to the back of my mind and focused on my partner. All of my worries and fears fell to the floor one by one as he spun me throughout the dance and kicked far away with my own feet.

I arched my back in Alex's arms when he dipped me on the final harsh note of the music, hanging in a dramatic pose until he pulled me up. He kissed the back of my hand again as our audience applauded for us.

"Alright!" I clapped my hands together, feeling infinitely more myself after leaving everything on the dancefloor. "We'll teach you the basic steps on your own first and then you can all partner up."

I did well to avoid Ian's eyes, though I couldn't help but glance over every so often when he wasn't looking. It didn't come as a surprise when the adoring woman chose him as her partner.

His pained expression almost brought me a sadistic joy, but I had to draw the line when her wandering hands landed on his butt. I took pity on him as he tried to create some distance while still being polite. I made my way over to them after telling the couple I was instructing to keep up the good work.

"May I step in for a minute?"

"Must you?" The woman gave a dreamy sigh. She looked longingly up at Ian from her short stature.

With a tight smile, I parted the two of them with my hands on their shoulders. "Alex!"

He came right over to us and I noticed how Ian tensed at his presence.

"While I help Ian, can you give this lovely woman the experience of a tango with a real man?" I leaned over and whispered to him, "And proper hand placement for a lady."

Understanding flashed across his features before he grinned at her. "It would be an honor."

"Well, you're quite the upgrade," the woman winked and let him sweep her away for a few minutes.

"You're getting the steps all wrong," I stated to Ian as we moved into position.

"I was too busy trying not to get groped," he muttered stiffly, looking down to follow my steps.

"I'm sorry," I told him genuinely. "I should have come over here sooner. Why didn't you stop her?"

"I wasn't going to be rude and ruin your class."

"Wow," I found myself saying under my breath. "That's really sweet of you, but you don't have let her get away with what was practically sexual harassment."

He looked up at me from our feet, coming to a stand still while I intertwined my legs through and around his own. I was guilty of doing more than the basic steps required, just so I could show off to him a little bit.

My last move was curling my leg around to the back of his, sliding it up his thigh and wrapping it around his hips. Then I brought it back down slowly, watching his Adam's apple bob as he swallowed before meeting his gaze. We starting moving again and he missed another step.

"Well, you didn't have to let him do what he did either."

I lifted a brow, "It's called dancing, Ian."

"This is dancing," he said as if he was convincing himself more than me. "That was...not."

A thrill ran through me as I realized why he was so sulky. "Are you jealous?"

He looked away and muttered, "No."

"Oh my god. You are jealous!"

The smile was wiped off my face when he sharply tugged me against him, melding our bodies together. The firm set of his jaw and the heat of his stare took the breath right out of me.

With a quick recovery, I instinctively threw my arms above my head in a move I knew about, but had never done with a partner.

I didn't know how he knew what to do-maybe he was following his own instincts-but I didn't care in that moment. His hands grazed from my wrists down my arms, the pressure increasing as his palms left a blazing trail from my waist to my hips. He spun me so my back was pressing against his chest.

Then he whispered in my ear, "I'm not jealous."

Yes, you are, I thought as Alex and the woman returned.

I was breathing like I just finished a quickstep and my heart was the beat for it.

And that wasn't dancing.

From then on, Ian's partner kept her hands in more appropriate places. Whatever Alex did or said to her seemed to work, but she looked disappointed to be dancing with Ian and she lit up anytime Alex passed by her.

The rest of the class went by without a hitch and all of the students were happy and worn out by the time it was over. A few came up to me afterwards and thanked me. One couple in particular told me I did an amazing job. They took the class for their 40th anniversary and hoped to see me again next year.

I was sweaty and exhausted, but I never felt so good or accomplished as I did after teaching a few people how to dance. Part of me wanted to jump around and squeal like a lunatic, but I held back since I wasn't alone or with Reyna.

"That was fantastic, Ferra," Alex said to me. "It has truly been a pleasure to work with you."

I smiled, bubbling up with pride. "Thank you."

Ian already had my duffle bag thrown over his shoulder. He said from the door, "We should get going, Ferret."

I saw the clock on the wall, gasping at how late it was already. With an apology and a short goodbye to Alex, we left the studio in a hurry. I still had to stop by my house to get a shower before we got on the road.

The odds of getting to the campsite before dark were dwindling and I actually started to feel glad that Ian stayed behind. He could be a fun travel buddy and it was nice not to be alone for the trip.

We were stopped at a traffic light and the radio was playing in the background to fill the silence.

"Thank you," I said, thinking about what he went through and everything he did for me.

The light turned green but Ian spared me a glance, "For what?"

"Just...thank you. I'm sorry for punching you." As an afterthought, I added, "And for the perverted grandma."

A few moments passed before he spoke again. "So does that mean you're done hating me today?"

I could never hate you, Ian Winters.

"There are quite a few hours left in the day, so we'll see."

"I can accept that," he smiled while keeping his eyes on the road. "Hey, do you mind if we stop by my house instead of yours? It's closer and I could use a quick shower too."

The last thing I wanted was to go on a five hour drive with a stinky, sweaty guy. And he always smelled incredible after a shower; I knew that because of the many sleepovers with Reyna. Catching a glimpse of him still wet from a shower was also a perk, along with a very rare towel-only sighting when he forgot to take his clothes to the bathroom with him.

I blamed him for triggering my boy craziness, but it was like trying to find a better guy and falling short every time.

It would be too easy for him if I readily agreed, so I considered my options until I remembered that I didn't pack a sweater for the chilly nights.

"Only if I can steal a hoodie for the weekend."

He sighed, ever reluctant to loan out any of his precious collection.

"Fine."

!

7 | Shorts

"You're wearing that on the camping trip?"

I frowned, searching my outfit for faults that didn't exist. I wore a short-sleeved shirt with the bedazzled khaki shorts I spent all night on, finishing the look with my hiking boots. As I resumed drying my hair with a towel, I asked him, "What's so wrong with it?"

"Short," was all Ian said.

"Shorts?"

"No, short. The shorts are...short."

"That's the point," I told him with a cheeky grin. I could have explained that I was taking a stand against my father and khaki pants in general, but Ian's appalled expression was too good to pass up.

"Aren't you worried about mosquitos? O-or bears?"

"Bug repellent. And I don't think bears are specifically attracted to legs." I smirked, "You seem to be though."

He opened his mouth to deny it, but he decided against it and turned his back to me. "You're right. Bears don't like skinny little Ferret legs."

My hair was as dry as it was going to get, so I threw the wet towel at him with a vengeance. It hit his back and fell to the floor in a heap. I sat down on his bed, crossing my arms as I watched him pull clothes from his dresser.

Ian admitted to me once we got to his house that he still needed to pack. He had to find his family's misplaced tents last night and loaded the car for his mom and sister, so he didn't get a chance to do it then. He could have done it while I was at the dance studio, but when I told him that, he shrugged me off and said he forgot about it.

I examined my surroundings while I waited for him to finish up. I spent a lot of time at their house, but I was rarely ever in Ian's room. Reyna was always with me the few times I had been in here, so I made it a point not to seem too interested in his personal space.

It was a bit messy with a few items of clothing strewn on the floor, but it wasn't too bad. In the corner of the room, there was a punching bag hanging from a hook in the ceiling, no doubt a contributor to his strong physique. Aside from the shelves, the most prominent on the teal walls were a classic truck poster and an 'Eat. Sleep. Game.' decal with an image of a controller above his bed.

I was sitting on a green plaid duvet with white sheets beneath it, and the queen bed itself was comfortable. The pine dresser was across from me beside the open closet and it had about ten hoodies hanging inside, along with a few dress shirts and pants. The suit he wore when he took Reyna to our Spring Formal was in the corner.

I smiled softly at my favorite memory of the night.

Ian practically marched over to me and my friend, Richie, during the last dance. When he asked to cut in, I had to mask my surprise at his boldness.

My heart skipped more beats than Ian's feet. Being that close to him with his arms around me was enough compensation for having my own feet stepped on.

I only wished he would take the initiative more often.

With a resigned sigh at the dead end of Memory Lane, I tried to choose which hoodie I wanted from my spot on the bed. Ian came over and put a backpack down beside me, then he started stuffing his clothes into it carelessly.

His hair was still wet from the quick shower he took before me, making the golden color a few shades darker. His white shirt clung to him like a second skin, slightly damp in areas where he must have missed in his rush to dry off.

I jumped to my feet, moving away from him to his closet. Clicking my tongue idly, I shuffled through the hoodies and paused on a black one with a spray-painted graphic on the front.

"You can't have Venom."

Rolling my eyes, I shoved it aside and caught sight of a yellow hoodie.

I asked, "Then what about Pikachu?"

"No," he responded as he zipped the bag up.

"Galaxy? It's too pretty for you, anyway."

I heard Ian take an exasperated breath and he came to stand half behind, half beside me. My shoulder was pressed against his chest as he reached around me to the hangers. He froze with his arm midair and, from the corner of my eye, I saw him angle his head toward me.

He inhaled and his voice was a low murmur, "Ferret?"

I kept my lips sealed, but acknowledged, "Hmm?"

"Did you use my shampoo?"

"It was either raspberry sorbet or grapefruit mint, I only chose the latter." I tried to be nonchalant with a shrug, "Didn't know it was specifically yours."

So totally knew it.

"Uh huh. The color should've given it away," he said, referring to how vibrantly colored Reyna's shampoo was, much like her dyed red hair.

"Sorry?" Not sorry.

"I never said it was a bad thing. It just surprised me."

Oh. I decided to tease him a little and smiled, "So you like me smelling like you?"

"Better me than my sister."

I tilted my head slightly, unsure what to make of that comment. I spared him a glance, but I didn't glean anything because he was focused on skimming through his hoodies. He seemed to be taking the task of finding one for me far too seriously.

"So," I broke the silence, "which one can I have?"

"Borrow," he corrected gruffly as he pulled one from the rack. "You can borrow this one."

He pushed the dark grey clothing into my hands and took the one next to it for himself. Mine had two boxing gloves on it with the words 'Total Knockout' above them, while his just had 'Killin' It' in a rectangle outline on the front. I liked his a bit more, but I didn't complain as I tied it around my waist. A thought struck me so I spun on my heel and browsed through the rest of the hoodies hanging in his closet.

"Hey, what happened to the ones that had things like 'FBI: Female Body Inspector,'" I mocked, "and 'FCK all I need is U' on them?"

"I like to call that my High School Collection." Ian sighed wistfully but then he shrugged it off, "I got rid of them."

"Well, look who else seems to be growing up," I smiled at him.

I saw Ian with a lot of girls throughout high school, but none of the relationships were serious. Pretty, bitchy, and ditzy was his type and he tended to lose interest in them quickly. Yet would always manage to end on good terms with the girls he dated, so very few (if any) hated him. All the boys worshipped the ground he walked on because of their own perverted assumptions.

Ian wasn't the type to sleep around though, and no one could say he wasn't genuine when he pursued a girl and started dating her.

He was the definition of a nice guy with the subtext of a player.

"Ready to go?" Ian asked, throwing the backpack over his shoulder.

I nodded, following him out of his room and then the house.

"Are you sure we should take your truck? My car is in better shape," I said, looking warily at the old red truck. "It is a very long drive..."

"Ferret, this truck is more reliable than any vehicle ever made," he exaggerated. "I use it every year for this trip, and I'm not going to lose faith in it now."

"I guess you're right." I sighed as I took one last look at the so-called reliable vehicle, then I climbed into the passenger side.

Ian wasn't right.

He was so far from right that he was more wrong than any person ever born, and that wasn't an exaggeration.

The first few hours were great. We had the windows down and it was a beautiful day for a scenic drive. We stopped at a gas station to fill up on fuel and get snacks to eat on the way there. The music was up until I convinced him to play a couple of games with me out of boredom.

We were playing a round of Kiss, Marry, Kill when it happened.

The irony of that game was like a slap in the face:

In the past, I wanted to marry him.

An hour ago, I still wanted to kiss him.

Now I just wanted to kill him.

Very. Painfully.

"Try again," I ordered after a few minutes of sitting in silence.

"I did try. Five times," Ian said, resting his forehead on the steering wheel. "There's no reception out here."

I glared at the 'X' on the top corner of my screen, hoping for just two bars to appear.

"I can't believe you don't have the tools to put the spare tire on."

"Well, I can't believe I ran over a nail in the middle of nowhere. These are newer tires. I didn't plan on getting a flat, you know."

I threw my head back against the cushion in exasperation. "Nobody plans to get a flat tire, Ian! It just happens!"

"I can see that you're upset—"

I interrupted him with a humorless laugh.

"—but it'll be okay, Ferret. I'm sure someone will drive by soon and help us. It's not like we're stranded out here."

So we waited.

And waited.

We were in the bed of his truck, still waiting as the sky turned to dusk. I was laying on my back with my feet dangling off the edge. Ian was sitting beside me with his fist against his temple as he watched for cars.

We were only a little over an hour away from the campsite, surrounded by nothing but trees and deserted, curving roads. The air was humid, but beginning to cool.

"This is getting ridiculous," I said after I sat up to stretch my aching back.

Ian ran a hand through his sandy hair. I rarely ever saw him stressed out, but that was a clear sign that he was on his way to Stressville. "We can sleep here tonight. I'm sure someone will come through in the morning."

"Or..." I trailed off, my gaze moving to the forest in thought for a minute. "We're close to the campsite, maybe only two hours or so walking distance if we cut through there."

"I thought I was the stupid one," Ian said, looking at me like I was boarding the crazy train.

"You are, but I happen to be desperate right now and that overshadows your stupidity," I explained as I hopped off of the tailgate.

"And why are you so desperate to go?" He crossed his arms, "My truck is safer than the woods."

"You also said it was reliable. I don't sleep well in a vehicle and this hunk of junk isn't comfortable," I motioned to the bed of the truck. "I see no reason not to go where I can have a tent and my own sleeping bag."

Ian shook his head.

"We might even make it in time for s'mores."

He scoffed and gave me a disapproving glance.

"We know this forest like the back of our hands." Hoping to convince him, I went on to list the reasons why it wasn't a stupid idea. "It's not even dark yet, but we have flashlights and a compass. Somewhere in your small brain you have the survival skills my dad taught you, and I know my fair share too. I'm also naturally good with directions."

"Like any Ferret should be," Ian smirked before his mouth fell back into a frown. "Look, it's not safe."

"Fine then," I muttered, slipping on the hoodie. I grabbed my bag from behind me and turned towards the woods. "You stay here where it's safe. I'm going camping."

Sitting still and waiting to be rescued wasn't in my blood. I was confident in my ability to find the campsite, even more so with Ian's help. I walked slow, counting each step until he joined me because I knew he would do it.

"Dammit, wait for me!" He called out.

I smiled, stopping in my tracks as Ian retrieved his backpack. It was twice the size of mine and had his sleeping bag attached to it. Travelling on foot with that thing weighing on his shoulders wasn't going to be easy. I was glad that I packed light for once.

He sidled up beside me and said, "This is a bad idea."

8 | Toasted Marshmallows

8 | Toasted Marshmallows

~ ☁ ☀ ☁ ~

"It should be right here," I huffed as I studied the map.

We had been walking for what felt like hours with no campsite or any sign of human life in sight. It was just us, an owl high up in a tree somewhere, and crickets mocking us in the distance.

Ian held the flashlight beam over the paper for me to see it. "I said you were looking at it wrong."

"Yes, but you're never right and I usually am," I argued in a weary tone.

As the night dragged on and our feet dragged even farther, my insults were losing their bite upon delivery. Like I forgot to put breathing holes in the boxes and they arrived lifeless to him. I wished my feet were dead too so they wouldn't ache anymore.

"I was right about this being a bad idea," he countered, sounding just as tired as me.

I closed my eyes, letting my arm and the useless map I was holding fall to my side. With a defeated sigh and no decent comeback because what he said was true, I apologized.

"I'm sorry. As much as it pains me to admit it, you were right. We would have been better off if we stayed with the truck."

"New plan," Ian clapped, startling me out of my thoughts. He must have scared the owl too, because there was a rustling of leaves and then a sudden silence above us.

I wondered where his sudden burst of energy came from and didn't exactly welcome it. If he saw my scowl, he made no indication of it.

"We'll set up camp here and continue on in the morning. And this time," he flashed the light in my face, "you're listening to me."

"Oh, wow," I uttered dryly, shoving his hand and the blinding beam away, "Ian Winters taking charge. I never thought I'd see the day."

He gave me a look that rivalled my tone before he unattached the sleeping bag from his backpack. He tossed the rolled fabric at me and

I caught it in my arms. I should have let it fall, but reflexes surpassed sass in my current state of exhaustion.

"Sit down and rest," he ordered. "I'm going to get some firewood."

"Damn, you're already making me hot enough without a fire."

Ah, there was my sass.

Ian stumbled over something on the ground, muttering a curse as he walked away. I smirked at his retreating back, feeling a little bit of myself returning at the prospect of sitting down.

While he was gone, I unrolled the sleeping bag and folded it in half for extra cushioning. Getting off of my sore feet was an incredible feeling, so I leaned back on my elbows and looked up at the stars with a smile on my face. For the first time since we started our journey into the forest, I took a deep, appreciative breath, filling my lungs with fresh and clean air.

The peace that was slowly making me relax was rudely interrupted by my growling stomach. I put an arm to my abdomen and curled my lip at the noisy sound. Taking a water bottle out of my duffel bag, I sipped on it to take the edge off. The snacks I had on the drive earlier didn't stay with me for long, but I didn't realize how hungry I was until now.

Side-eyeing Ian's backpack, I gave in and tugged it closer to see if he had any proteins bars in there. Unzipping one compartment of the bag, I dug my hand in and found his clothes and three water bottles. It seemed like he came prepared, so my anticipation rose as I tried another zipper.

When I made a blessed discovery, I thought I died of starvation and went straight to heaven.

I nearly cried tears of joy as I pulled the bag out.

"Marshmallows!"

"And that is why I still call you Ferret." Ian came over with his arms full of fallen branches and twigs. He set the pile down in the middle of our little campsite and continued, "Because you still act like one."

"It's called foraging and it's an instinct of all living creatures when they're starved," I defended with narrowed eyes.

Yet I still reached into his backpack again to see what other treasures could be found. My mouth watered for the packages of jerky and walnuts, so I took those out too. There were a few protein bars, but they were far less appetizing in comparison.

"Whatever helps you sleep at night," he grinned down at me as he brushed his hands off.

"Just shut up and build a fire," I muttered bitterly and looked down to tear into a piece of beef jerky. That was how I chose to mask the way his moonlit smile affected me.

While I grazed on the dried meat and walnut halves, I watched Ian gather rocks from around the clearing and arrange them in a circle. My gaze unabashedly followed his every move as he set up the fire, since he was too distracted with the task at hand to notice me.

I forgot all about food and started drooling over the snack in front of me: Ian snapping branches in half like they were nothing more than toothpicks.

If it wasn't a full moon, I would have had a harder time seeing such a glorious sight. The muscles in his arms flexed before each break, then the tension released after and he tossed the broken wood into a new pile.

With a distracted swallow, I didn't realize there was still a half-chewed piece of jerky in my mouth and started choking.

Tears filled my eyes because the jerky scratched my throat on its way down, but fortunately it wasn't lodged there. I grabbed my water bottle and drank until the sharp feeling was gone. It was only when I was able to breathe properly that my mind registered the hand rubbing soothing circles on my back. I looked over my shoulder to see Ian crouched down with a look of concern.

"You alright there, Ferret?" He asked, tilting his head down at a better angle to check me over. "Ate too fast?"

"No," I said, my gaze drawn to his lips. "I'm fine."

He was close.

So close I could easily kiss him just to feel his lips on mine one more time. The problem was that Reyna wasn't around to dare me, so I had no excuse to fall back on. No reason other than I simply wanted to do it. Then with a jolt, it occurred to me that I was quiet for too long and turned away before he caught me staring.

I spouted off my belated answer to his question, "I choked on shrapnel from a branch."

Now that was stupid of me, but I had no choice other than to run with it. I couldn't have just said that it was a piece of jerky and omitted the part about drooling over him. That would have required too much brain power and I didn't have enough to spare after such a long night.

"Must you insist on being such a caveman? Pick up shorter branches next time like normal people."

He exhaled a disbelieving laugh at my prickliness, "I'm not a caveman! I was just in a hurry to get back so I wasn't picky." Then he feebly added, "It's scary out there alone in the dark."

I snorted and opened my mouth to retort.

"I also didn't want to leave you alone any longer than necessary."

My jaw clamped shut. That was sweet-

"You would have eaten everything before I got back."

I twisted around to unleash my fury on him in the form of my fist, but he dove out of my reach right before the impact.

It wasn't my intention to forgive him so soon for being an ass, but the fire crackling a couple of minutes later was admittedly nice. It was a comfort to have the light, and I felt like I could finally relax after hours of stress. Ian knew what to do to survive in the woods, more so than me anyway. I had a few survival skills of my own, but making a safe campfire wasn't one of them.

With a victorious smile, Ian sat down beside me. I scooted over to make more room for him on the folded sleeping bag, but our knees were still touching in the limited space. He picked up two sticks that he set aside earlier and unsheathed a knife from his backpack. I curiously watched him as he whittled one, making a sharp point at the end. He handed it to me wordlessly and did the same to the other stick.

Once I understood what they were for, I reached for the marshmal-lows and tore the bag open. I picked out two that weren't squished

and gave him one of them, then we stabbed the centers with our sticks and held them out near the fire. We sat there in companionable silence waiting for our marshmallows to puff up and turn brown.

Then Ian chuckled.

"What?" I asked, rotating the stick. I didn't move my eyes away from the marshmallow in fear of burning it.

"Just remembering when I taught you and Reyns how to toast marshmallows," he explained, the nostalgic smile evident in his tone.

I found myself smiling at the memory too.

It was the second summer of our families camping together. Reyna and I were ten years old, while Ian was twelve. Reyna and I kept burning our marshmallows-most often because they caught on fire-and they always turned out black and tasting like smoke. It reached the point where Reyna started whining and begged Ian to help us. He had been eating his fill of the perfectly toasted sugar pillows. He was weak to his little sister even then, so he taught us how to do it without much complaint.

I remember my cheeks blazing when Ian settled between us, but I was quick to blame it on the heat from the fire. He gave us each one marshmallow and took two for himself, then he instructed us to hold them down near the embers instead of over the flames. Reyna and I watched in amazement as our marshmallows puffed and started to brown without burning, as long we kept rotating them.

Reyna squealed in success and stuffed the whole marshmallow into her mouth, piping hot and molten inside. I wanted mine darker, but I made the mistake of looking to see how my friend's turned out. Just those few extra seconds was all it took for mine to catch on fire.

"I still remember the completely defeated look on your face," Ian recalled with a grin.

"Who wouldn't be defeated after ruining a perfect marshmallow? I really wanted it," I defended with a slight pout.

"You were pouting kind of like that too," Ian said, pointing to my bottom lip. "I thought it was cute."

Whoa. Calm down, heart. We were little kids back then.

"It still is," he added in an undertone, almost bashfully as he focused back on the fire.

There was no calming my heart after that comment. I cleared my throat, diving back into the past so I didn't have to cope with the present, "So is that why you gave me one of your marshmallows? Because you thought I was cute?"

I remembered being utterly smitten when he held out the skewered marshmallows to me, offering the top one. With a quiet thanks, I pulled it off with my little fingers and ate it. It was the best toasted marshmallow I ever had, and I thought so even now.

He gave me a noncommittal shrug. "I didn't like to see you sad and I was worried you might cry. Reyna used to cry over small things, and it killed me every time. I'd do whatever it takes not to see her cry. I guess I feel the same way about you."

He seemed lost in his thoughts again, and I didn't know what to say to bring him back to me. The mood dropped for the both of us as he undoubtedly returned to thinking of his sister getting older and not needing him anymore. I didn't like being filed into the sibling category, but even more so hated that he was having a difficult time.

We were on our third round of marshmallows when I finally spoke up.

"Ian," I started, putting the stick aside and staring into the flames so I could concentrate on my words. "Just because Reyna isn't a kid anymore doesn't mean she won't always be your little sister. It just means that you have let her be an adult too. Let her make her own decisions and be there for her when they turn out to be mistakes. Yeah, she might cry once in a while, but you will always be there to wipe her tears and beat up the idiot who caused them. Hell, I'll help you do it. No one messes with my best friend."

I heard a small chuckle.

Then I continued, "You filled the shoes of a father when your dad left you guys. On top of being a son and a brother, which is pretty damn incredible. You taught Reyna how to take care of herself, so you need to trust and believe in her because you've done a great job being her older brother and someone she knows she can depend on."

"I think you're the first person to tell me that," Ian said quietly. A few moments passed before he added, "Thank you, Ferra."

I smiled softly when he used my real name instead of Ferret. "You should be thinking about how to get us unlost tomorrow, not worrying about her. She's probably eating s'mores or snoring in her tent right about now."

After a long moment, he admitted, "I wasn't thinking about her."

I moved my gaze from the fire to him. The bright flames were mesmerizing, but they couldn't compare to his eyes. I felt his stare while I was talking, but my breath hitched at the unexpected intensity in it. I noticed how close we were again, but neither of us seemed willing to move away.

"You know," his voice was low but still heard over the sound of the crackling fire, "you can depend on me too."

I felt that familiar pang in my chest. "I don't need a brother, Ian. I told you I can take care of myself."

He shook his head slowly, his eyes darting so quickly to my lips that I almost missed it. Even still, I wondered if it was trick of the firelight and dancing shadows until his words cleared all doubt from my mind.

"Not as a brother."

I didn't know if he drew closer or if there was only an inch between us to begin with. All I knew was that I wanted that inch to be nonexistent.

"Then..." I was afraid to ask, but did it anyway. "As a friend?"

As soon as the question left my mouth, he answered it by pressing his lips against mine.

His kiss was tentative, like he was testing the waters and expecting me to push him away. Little did he know that wasn't in the realm of possibilities for me.

At finally being able to feel his addictively soft lips again, a sound of satisfaction escaped me as I didn't just fall into the kiss, but into him too.

He took that as a sign of encouragement and wrapped his arms around my waist. He lifted me onto his lap, so I leaned against him and hooked my ankles around his back.

I couldn't stop touching him with thoughts of 'Finally' echoing through my mind. My hands glided across the muscles in his arms and up to his shoulders, into his hair and back down to his chest. His palms slid up my bare legs, distracting me from my own exploration until his tongue ran across my lip. I waited so long for him, I was going to make him work for it. I didn't expect Ian to retaliate when I refused to open up to him.

One of his hands ran up the back of my thigh, higher over the fabric of my shorts, and then he gently squeezed. It was a teasing warning that had me gasping in surprise.

He took full advantage of throwing me off guard and pushed his tongue into my mouth. The sweet and smoky flavor of toasted marshmallows was intoxicating, so I pressed back for more than just a taste and was rewarded with a pleased groan from him.

It was a choreography of our own; a dance of lips and tongues. Twirling. Dipping. Caressing. Parting for a breath, before playing the song again. Neither of us were beginners or experts to the type of dance, but new to the emotions evoked by each other.

"Ian," I sighed contentedly on the third breath.

I used to wonder what it would be like if he ever kissed me. I imagined he would be sweet and tender, but I never imagined he had a passionate side too. I thought I would be the assertive one, and I usually was when kissing a boy, but even I was having a hard time keeping up with him. It was almost as if he had waited as long as me.

I dared to hope, but realized how wrong I was a moment later when he pushed me away.

"I'm sorry."

I was in a daze that shattered when those two words registered and he moved me off of his lap.

"I got caught up in the moment. I shouldn't have-"

"Don't," I warned, sharply cutting him off.

I hated that my legs were wobbly when I stood up. My heart ached, more so than it ever had over Ian. It was different than watching him with other girls, different than not being noticed by him. It hurt so much more because he kissed me and instantly regretted it.

It was a slap in the face.

Rejection at its finest.

I didn't want to hear his excuses or apologies. I should have expected it from him, because he was what he had always been; A predictable, reliable idiot.

I couldn't handle the look of pity on his face when I felt a hot tear burn a trail down my cheek.

My emotions were a flurry and I couldn't think straight, but I had just one thought coming through as he kept fumbling for what to say.

I needed to get away from him.

So I left him calling for me as I ran into the woods, because getting more lost seemed like a better alternative to staying with Ian. Was it stupid? Yes, but I at least tried to go in a single direction and planned to go just far enough away to create some distance for a little while.

I left everything behind, including my flashlight. So I didn't see the thick tree root ahead of me and tripped, falling straight to ground. I groaned more out of frustration than pain, squeezing my scraped hands into fists before pushing to my feet.

The grumbling sound of a wild animal made me freeze in fear.

Unshed tears blurred my vision, but I could still see the bear moving closer to me.

9 | SLEEPING BAG

9 | Sleeping Bag

The bear paused in its approach, but by then there was a mere eight feet left between us. It stood on its hind legs and sniffed the air curiously. I would have thought the bear was cute if I wasn't at risk of being mauled by it.

It didn't appear to be threatened by me yet, so I started to breathe again with a slow exhale. Though it did nothing to calm my rapid heart rate and I had to ignore my instinct to turn and run from the danger.

"Hi there." Talking was probably a bad idea, but I proceeded to ramble quietly anyway. "I just made out with a guy I've liked for ages and he said it was a mistake, so I'm having a really bad night. I would appreciate it if you don't kill me. I suppose if you do, he'll have to live with my death for the rest of his life. It would be fun to haunt him—"

"Ferra!"

My eyes widened at the loud call of my name, but I didn't look away from the bear because it dropped back down to all fours.

Ian the Idiot appeared by my side, out of breath and angry. "What the hell were you thinking running into the middle of the woods?! It's not safe!"

"Shut the hell up, idiot," I said, keeping my tone soft and sweet.

He blinked at me, then turned his head to look at what I was staring at, "Oh, crap."

"Yeah, not the best idea to yell in front of a bear, you freaking idiot."

"What do we do?" he whispered, moving closer to me and angling his body to face the bear completely.

"You're asking me? I thought you were the expert out here."

"I don't remember what your dad taught me about bears," he responded, adopting his own non-threatening tone. "You do different things for different ones, I think."

"So helpful," I clenched my teeth.

The bear growled, no longer pacified by our voices. I blamed Ian entirely.

"Okay," my voice shook. I tried to recall the same knowledge my dad instilled in me. I thought it was mostly useless information, like what are the odds of running into a bear. Then again, I never expected to be in the current situation.

"We can't run, I know that for sure."

Then Ian supplied, "Can't turn our backs either."

"Sideways." My heart leaped as I remembered one option to get away, and we could only hope it was the right one. "We move slowly and carefully sideways until we're out of sight."

Ian grasped my elbow and guided me to his other side. "You go first."

"No, we have to do it together. Come on." Taking his hand, I ordered softly, "Follow my lead."

While the bear stayed where it was, I side-stepped once and Ian did the same after me.

"There's a tree root sticking up here," I warned, using my feet to feel around since I had to keep my eyes on the bear. "Be careful."

Ian squeezed my hand, fumbling with his foot to find the root and step over it. When he did, I commended him and took another step.

It was like trying to teach him how to dance, but with a hungry bear as our audience. The guy had two left feet and it was made worse by the fact that he couldn't look down.

"I've got us," I assured him with a wave of confidence as we put more distance between us and the bear.

Then the bear had to ruin it by growling again.

Ian and I froze. We stared wide-eyed, like deer caught in headlights, as the bear charged at us.

At the last second, Ian wrapped his arms around me and turned so his back was a shield to the impending attack. My eyes snapped shut when I heard the thuds of the bear's paws hitting the ground as it got closer.

There was a resounding roar.

Then nothing.

I still heard the pounding steps of the bear, but they were fading past us.

"Ian?"

He hadn't released me from his death grip and it was beginning to hurt.

He responded with high-pitched and strained, "Yeah?"

I would have sighed but my lungs were being crushed, so I had to settle with an eye roll. "You can let go now."

"Is it gone?"

"Yes."

"It's not a ninja bear waiting to strike?"

"No."

"We're not going to die?"

"Yes."

"Yes?!"

"No! No, we are not going to die." Then I hissed, "But you will if you don't let me go."

Ian finally let go of me and stepped away. We looked around to confirm that the bear really was gone and it was true; we were alone in the forest again and quite possibly lost. Back to square one, but now without our bags and supplies.

"You were that scared, but you were still willing to be my meat shield?"

"Of course," he scoffed like he didn't just risk his life to save mine. "And can you not say that, please? It's too soon."

Before I could thank him or say anything else, Ian moved ahead of me and turned on his flashlight.

"Let's get back to our camp before our new friend decides to visit us again."

"How exactly do you plan to—" I stopped mid-sentence when he picked up a shirt from the ground and threw it over his shoulder.

He kept walking, so I hurried to catch up to him. A few feet further, he collected a pair of pants.

"You left a trail of...clothes?"

"Yep," he answered, adding a second shirt to the pile forming on his shoulder.

I snorted and covered my mouth, but it didn't do much to muffle the outburst of laughter that bubbled up from my throat. I didn't know why it was so funny to me, but it may have had to do with the adrenaline rush and exhaustion. He made a smart decision though, as much as I loathed to admit it.

He nudged me forward, shaking his head at my hysterics. I laughed harder when he retrieved a pair of boxers. I found it all so entertaining that time flew by and we were back at our little campsite.

Ian went over to his backpack and shoved all of his clothes back into it. He must have put the fire out before he came to find me. The realization of how utterly stupid I was to run off caused me to sober up. My smile faded into an ashamed frown as I watched Ian spread out his sleeping bag.

I hesitated, "I'm sorry for running."

"You should be sorry," he interjected in a mutter. "It was stupid and extremely dangerous."

My gaze dropped to my feet.

"But I don't blame you for choosing the company of a bear over me."

I bit my lip as the smile returned.

"Now I know I'm not a cuddly bear, but at least I won't bite."

His words confused me until I looked up.

Ian was in his sleeping bag, laying on his side in a paint-me-like-one-of-your-French-girls pose. He patted the spot in front of him, inviting me to join him.

"No," I said. "Not gonna happen."

"We don't really have a choice in the matter, unless you want me to sleep on the cold, hard ground after saving your life."

"Excuse me. I recall saving both of our lives, Mr. 'What do we do? I don't know what to do,'" I mocked.

"Fine," he said after a minute. "I can't deny that, but it doesn't change the fact that we have to share the sleeping bag. It is technically mine and I'm sharing it with you."

"You're so kind, Ian," I stated dryly.

"Thank you, Ferret. I do try."

With a heavy sigh, I slid in beside him and zipped it up. The sleeping bag was spacious for one person, but there was barely enough room for two. I had my back to Ian and he was practically breathing down my neck.

He cleared his throat and attempted to shift away from me, but his movements pulled on the sleeping bag. I closed my eyes as I waited for him to get comfortable and stop moving, grounding my teeth together when I felt another tug.

He eventually settled when we were back-to-back and I found myself relaxing too. The warmth radiating from the back of his body pressing against mine was comforting after what we just went through. I could feel the muscles in his shoulder blades flex as he adjusted his arms and I enjoyed the moment of us being so close. It wasn't likely to happen again after what happened between us and the blatant rejection.

A lump formed in my throat when I was reminded of why I ran away in the first place, yet I was grateful that we seemed to have a mutual understanding of not mentioning it.

"Thank you," I said to him.

"For what?"

"For protecting me."

"Always." His voice vibrated through my back directly to my heart. "And thank you too."

"For?"

"Saving us."

A small smile lifted one side of my mouth.

"I knew you were an amazing dancer," he continued, "but that was good footwork back there."

"You haven't really seen me dance, so you can't say I'm amazing."

"Yes, I have," Ian declared.

With a heavy dose of doubt, I asked, "When?"

"Your last recital."

I blinked a few times, my tired gaze landing on a tree a few feet away from me. The last dance recital I was a part of was a few months ago. I was the lead with a guy I thought I liked and we went on a double-date with Reyna and Wesley. I had no idea that Ian was there.

"I knew Reyna was going on a date, so I kind of...followed her and Wesley. I don't trust a guy who drives an old Mustang, especially him," he muttered. "Anyway, I didn't know they were going to your recital since, you know, I wasn't invited to it."

I almost laughed when he sounded offended. It was cute, but still came as a surprise. I didn't think he cared enough to go, and I couldn't imagine how nervous I would have been had I known he was in the audience.

"I went home after it was over." As an afterthought, he added, "I'm just lucky Reyna didn't catch me."

I did chuckle then. I should have told him how wrong it was to stalk his sister and her date, but I wasn't going to ruin the moment. Especially after what he said next.

"It was worth it to see you," he yawned.

It took me a minute to respond, maybe because I needed to build up the courage to say it.

"Maybe I'll invite you next time."

"I'd like that," were the last words he whispered before he fell asleep.

I closed my eyes, "Me too."

10 | SKIPPING STONES

1
0 | Skipping Stones

~☁☀☁~

Birds chirping their morning songs.

An arm draped over me, tightening around my waist and pulling me closer to a wall of warmth against my back.

Steady, soft puffs of air tickling my neck.

A quiet hum of contentment in my ear.

Then the distinctive sound of a camera.

"Revenge is sweeter than Skittles," a familiar voice uttered with glee.

"They're waking up," a deeper voice warned. Then a pause. "What are you doing?"

"Taking a video. It's so much better than a pic. Amateurs."

I opened my eyes, blinking the restful sleep away. My groggy mind cleared enough to notice that I was face-to-phone, and my best friend was behind the lens. Her bright red hair and evil grin peeked out at me.

"I call this documentary 'Homo Sapiens Spooning in the Wild.'"

Wesley coughed from where he stood next to her, "That doesn't sound like a documentary, Reyna."

There was a dazed mumble about spoons and cereal behind me and then I felt something biting my hair.

The realization was like having a shot of espresso injected directly into my bloodstream. I tried to sit up, but a strong arm yanked me back down with a grumbled protest. I gaped when a nose burrowed against the skin between my neck and shoulder with a long inhale.

"Aww, he doesn't want to let go of his snuggly ferret," Reyna cooed as they watched the scene unfold.

"Ian!" I snapped just as I felt the lightest brush of his lips.

He woke up with a start and cried, "Is it a bear?! I didn't eat your porridge, I swear!"

"Shut up, Goldilocks," I groaned, finally able to shove his heavy arm off of me.

Ian sat up, squinting at Reyna and Wesley. Then after a yawn, he blinked and looked at me, "Are they real?"

"Unfortunately," I muttered, getting to my feet. "How did you guys find us?"

Reyna laughed at my question, so Wesley filled us in on the joke.

"We're on a hike. You guys are only about twenty minutes from the campsite."

"You're kidding, right?"

He shook his head with the ghost of a smirk. Wesley found it just as amusing as his girlfriend did, but he had the decency to be more discreet than her.

Once Reyna stopped cackling, she wiped her tears and asked how we got lost in the woods.

I told them about the flat tire and our adventure with the bear last night while Ian rolled up the sleeping bag. I obviously wasn't going to bring up the kiss, but it was obvious to Reyna that some details were left out. She didn't draw attention to it, but she did give me a 'we'll talk later' look.

With everything packed up, they led us to the campsite.

The tents were all set up in the surrounding area and I couldn't wait to sleep inside one of them, safe from bugs, bears, and big idiots. There was a fire pit in the center with extra wood and a few folding chairs placed around it. Two large coolers and sealed bags of nonperishable food were in the corner by a picnic table.

That was where my little sister and dad were sitting, but the mothers of our group must have been off on their own somewhere.

"Well, it's nice to see you aren't sick with worry over me," I announced my presence to my family.

"Mr. Glitter!" Meg squealed and ran past me to get to Ian.

He lifted her up into his arms, "Hey, munchkin."

She kissed his cheek and hugged him so they were cheek-to-cheek.

I rolled my eyes at my flirtatious little sister and walked over to my dad. He welcomed me with a warm smile, but it turned frigid when he saw what I was wearing.

"Really? First your little sister's pants and now yours? Did you have to cut them so short?! It's not practical or appropriate."

I forgot about the modifications Meg and I made to the khakis our dad so kindly gifted to us. He hadn't seen mine until now and his reaction did not disappoint.

"Careful there, dad. You're starting to sound like Ian," I teased.

He directed a glare at Ian and asked him, "Were you looking?"

"No, sir."

He did a lot more than just look, I thought as I met Ian's eyes. When I mouthed 'liar' to him, he turned away so I wouldn't see the blood rushing to his cheeks. Meg-ever the observant one when it came to hot guys-was eager to point it out.

"Mr. Glitter is blushing!" She giggled, "You're so cute!"

Ian shushed her and tried to brush it off with an awkward chuckle.

"So!" I clapped my hands together to draw everyone's attention away from him. "Where's breakfast?"

A protein bar was tossed at my face.

"Thanks, dad," I muttered.

"You're welcome, daughter," he grinned too brightly. "Meg and I were about to go to the lake to catch some dinner. Would you kids like to join us?"

"Please, please, please," Megan begged. Then she whispered loud enough for everyone to hear, "I don't wanna go fishing. He'll make me touch the worms."

"Bait," he corrected her with a dejected frown.

"They're still worms," Meg countered with her nose to the air. "And they're yucky. So will you guys please," she drew out the pleading word, "come with us?"

And that was how we found ourselves on the short trail to the lake. I was ready to curl up in my own sleeping bag while everyone else went, but I didn't want to miss out on any more of the trip.

"So tell me what you didn't tell me when we found you two," Reyna whispered to me.

I looked up from the ground to my dad and Ian walking ahead of us, with Wesley not far behind them. Meg was fortunate enough to get a piggyback ride from Ian, but I almost pitied him because he had to be just as tired as me without lugging her around.

My gaze fell to the slight strain of his muscles as he hoisted her higher. It was not fair that he could look so good sweaty like that while I felt disgusting and in great need of a shower.

"There's nothing to tell," I murmured back. Wesley could without a doubt hear us, but I was more worried about Ian. "Speaking of this morning, are you going to delete that video?"

"Nope! You never deleted the pictures of me and Wes while we were babysitting Meg. In fact, Wes uses one of them as a wallpaper on his phone because you sent them to him."

We heard a quiet confirmation from Wesley, who seemed far too amused by our exchange.

Seeking revenge for such a cute photoshoot, I thought as I remembered coming home to the two of them sound asleep in a blanket fort with Megan. "I don't see why you're complaining."

She grinned after she recovered from tripping over a tree root. "Same to you. There will be plenty of screenshots to choose from since it's a long video. I bet Ian would love to have a new wallpaper. "

I slowed my steps and threw my head back to the sky before looking to my best friend. She kept pace with me as we put more distance between us and the rest of the group. I gave in and admitted to her, "He kissed me. Like, really kissed me."

Reyna screamed.

Wesley was by her side in a split second and Ian with the monkey on his back was right behind him. My dad turned in our direction, but he didn't seem too concerned because of how often he heard us squealing over trivial things.

Reyna smiled at everyone staring at her as they waited for an explanation. "Spider. A really big spider. Like...massive."

Meg climbed up higher on Ian, who looked just as scared. She squeaked, "Where?"

"It's gone now, Sunshine," Reyna assured her. "It ran away when I screamed. Onwards, people!"

I waited until they were ahead of us again to speak. "Nice save."

"He kissed you?" She was back to whispering. "Was it just a peck on the lips or more?"

The look I gave her told her all she needed to know, but maybe not all she wanted to know.

She covered her mouth with both hands to muffle her excitement, then she asked, "So are you guys finally together now?"

"No. He regretted it. Then a bear almost ate us for a midnight snack."

Reyna's brows darted up under her red bangs, "What?"

I thought her reaction was due to the bear, but then she glared daggers at the back of Ian's head.

"I'm going to kill him."

I grabbed the back of her shirt when she lunged forward to follow through with it. The others were completely unaware of the silent battle going on behind them. Reyna was struggling to get out of my grip while I dodged her flailing limbs to get a better grip.

"Do it and I'll tell your boyfriend about your Fifty Shades of Wesley Black fantasy," I warned, coming up with it off the top of my head.

She stopped moving with a disgusted shudder, "That's not even true!"

"It doesn't have to be," I released her with a smirk.

Reyna heaved a sigh, "He's an idiot."

"The biggest."

"Bigger than the imaginary spider."

I smiled at the joke.

Our usual shortcut to the lake was a path less travelled, so we had to traverse an obstacle course of rocks-big and small-to reach the glistening water ahead of us. We could have gone around them, but it was easy enough to climb over to the flatter land.

Wesley was kind enough to take Reyna's hand and help her over the larger rocks because she was having difficulty with her short legs.

Then there was Meg who's feet didn't even touch the ground with Ian carrying her.

The lucky girls, I thought as I had no trouble on my own or a guy to fawn over me.

"Excuse me, miss."

The sudden appearance of someone at my side caused me to misstep on a rock. Just as I started to stumble, an arm wrapped around my waist and caught me.

"Falling for me already?"

I scoffed at the cliché line and looked up at the boy who made me lose my footing. He was around my age, kind of cute with short, spiked brown hair and green eyes.

"No," I told him, pushing out of his arms once I was stable. "I don't fall, I carry myself like a freaking queen."

He smiled at me then, revealing dimples that could offer the slightest redemption for his lame pickup line. "A queen has servants for that, you know."

He had a good point there.

"Allow me to be yours."

Just as I was about to ask what he meant, a surprised squeal escaped me when he effortlessly scooped me up.

I was used to being lifted by my dance partners, but with a stranger, I didn't trust that he wouldn't drop me. So I clung onto his neck when he started moving towards the lake.

"You okay back there, Ferret?" Ian called when he heard the sound I made and turned to see what happened. He stopped walking and watched us draw closer with a confused frown and narrowed eyes.

"Yeah, I'm good," I tried a confident smile as we passed him.

The stranger carrying me nodded once in greeting and grinned, "She's good."

I glanced over the boy's shoulder to Ian, who stood still like a statue with an expression as hard as stone.

Meg shouted towards me and in Ian's ear, "That boy is smoooooooth!"

The stranger chuckled and called back to her, "A.F, princess!"

Curiosity got the best of me, so I asked, "What does that mean?"

"I'm smooth as f-" he stopped, thought better of it after another glance at my sister, and showed off his dimples again. "Fudge."

Alright, he was pretty damn adorable. Although my eyes kept straying to Ian who slowly followed our steps with a deeper frown etched into his face. It didn't feel right being in another guy's arms right after that kiss, no matter the aftermath of it. There were still unspoken words between us and I didn't like leaving it that way.

The stranger noticed me staring behind us and glanced back. When he eased me down onto my feet after we made through to the other side, he asked, "Boyfriend?"

"What?" I looked at him, drawn from my thoughts. "Oh. No, he's not."

He seemed to think I was going to say more, so I attempted to lighten the mood and veer away from the complicated topic.

"He's just my little sister's servant." I played off of what he said.

"Ah," he smiled with a twinkle of understanding in his gaze. "The princess and her noble steed."

I laughed hard at that, feeling lighter than I had all morning. "Oh my god," I held the stitch in my side, gasping for air, "I think I needed that laugh. Thank you."

"It was my pleasure," he said like he knew I needed it. "I'll be here all weekend, so I hope I get to see your smile again...?"

"Ferra."

"Ferra," he echoed and started backing away. "Have a day as beautiful as you."

He didn't give me his name as he pivoted on his heels and walked off. He managed to make me feel better, even if he was cheesier than a block of cheddar. With a grin still on my face, I turned around to look for others and join them.

I jumped, startled by how close Ian was with a scowl and a giggling Megan on his back.

"Careful, Ian," I cautioned once I regained my composure. "Your jealousy is showing again."

"I'm not jealous," he argued halfheartedly, squatting down to let Meg off.

My little sister rolled her eyes when dad called her. "Dad," she whined as she ran to him, "it was just getting good!"

I patted Ian's shoulder as I sauntered past him to go to Reyna.

She and Wesley were standing near the edge of the lake trying to skip stones. He may have been an expert in chemistry, but he obviously wasn't so great with physics.

And neither is Reyna, I realized as she threw a stone with a bit too much force. It flew through the air and plopped into the water with a single splash.

"Do you mind?" My dad huffed at them. "You're scaring all the fish away."

Meg picked up a pebble and threw it into the water. "Maybe she's trying to save the fishies."

"Or kill them before you can," I snorted, earning a glare from Reyna. I draped my arm around her shoulder and said, "I bet Wesley agrees with me."

He lifted a sardonic brow, "That wouldn't be very smart of me."

Reyna nudged my arm off and wrapped both of hers around him, "Wes is a genius, you know."

Wesley met my gaze with a mischievous glint in his eyes. He undoubtedly agreed with me, but he looked like the cat that got the milk as he pulled her closer against him.

Sneaky, but still a genius, and I had to admit that I was a little impressed by it. My girl knew how to pick them.

If only I could too.

Sexy dumbass with a heart of gold was apparently my type.

"Well," I clapped my hands and rubbed them together, "if you two are done pelting the fish, do you want to go for a swim?"

Before either of them could answer, Meg shrieked. Our heads turned to her as she leaped up from the ground. "The worms are alive!"

"Not for long," our dad said.

"Because you're going to stab them with a hook!" She crossed her arms, "I won't do it and you can't make me."

"That's fine," his tone became sulky. "I wouldn't mind some peace and-"

He stopped mid-sentence and looked our way, Reyna and I taking a small step back from his next victim.

"Wesley! Come here, son. Let me teach you how to fish."

We tried not to laugh at the stricken look on Wesley's face. He questioned under his breath, "Can I say no?"

I shook my head. "He will hold it against you for the rest of your life. And by that I mean even if you outlive him, he will haunt you until the day you die."

"You're exaggerating."

With a tilt of my head, I asked, "Am I?"

Reyna gave the poor fellow a parting kiss and he trudged over to where my dad sat holding two fishing poles.

"If that scared him," she said as she watched him go, "I'm curious about how he's going to handle the spooky campfire stories."

I chuckled, "It's fact versus fiction, so he should be fine."

If he manages to survive my dad first...

11 | Picnic Table

1

1 | Picnic Table

~ ☁ ☀ ☁ ~

Reyna and I were sitting at a picnic table playing Nertz—a card game we've played since we were kids—when Wesley came over and sat down beside her. He had only been with my dad for almost two rounds of our game and I was surprised to see him so soon.

"You didn't last long," I said, putting a card down in one of the center piles before Reyna could get to it.

"His favorite fish is halibut," he commented as he watched us play, intrigued by the lesser known game.

"Ok...?"

"Nertz!" Reyna shouted as she put her last card down, earning a scowl from me while I collected the cards to count the points.

I defeated her the first time, but her winning streak had begun. It was hard to beat her because of how quick she could be, especially when she was on a sugar high.

"Your dad didn't like it when I told him how much mercury is in the average halibut." Wesley adjusted his glasses and smiled, "The final straw was when I went into detail about the health hazards related to mercury."

"You are brilliant," Reyna grinned, happy that her boyfriend got out of an afternoon away from her.

"Well, I'm not eating fish for dinner," I muttered, tossing him a pack of cards. We had an extra deck because Ian played with us when he was bored enough, but he was too busy keeping Meg out of trouble.

We explained the rules to Wesley and showed him how to play. He was pretty good for a newbie, but he was too slow and Reyna still won. He told her that he could probably beat her with some practice.

I choked back laughter and she just gave him an indulgent smile.

As we were about to start another round, our moms finally decided to make their first appearance of the day.

They forced us to vacate the picnic table in order to make room for them, the romance books they were giggling over, and a small cooler packed with sandwich essentials for lunch.

"Yeah, great to see you too, mom," I told my mom sarcastically after I motioned for Reyna and Wesley to go on without me.

"Oh, sweetie. Don't feel so dejected," she pulled me into a hug and smothered me with a kiss on the cheek. "I knew you would be safe with Ian, but I am very happy to see you. I just assumed your class ran late and you guys decided to drive out here this morning."

"Actually," I crossed my arms, "we got lost in the woods last night. And had a bear encounter, that we survived because of me."

Her eyes widened and the jaws of all three women dropped.

"Just so you know." I turned on my heels and walked away.

Maybe next time I would be shown a little more concern when I returned from the bear claws of death, unscathed to see another day.

My friends were already waiting for me at the end of the pier, while Ian and Meg were already in the water. We all wore swimsuits under our clothes in anticipation for a swim in the lake.

I almost laughed when I saw the goofy grin on Reyna's face when Wes took his glasses and shirt off. Instead of teasing her about her expression, he smiled and gave her a quick kiss before jumping into the water.

Meg, perched on Ian's shoulders, giggled and clapped above his head while he treaded water nearby. I was the last one in after Reyna, so I angled towards those two when I jumped, making a splash in their direction. The sight of my little sister clinging to Ian's head like a baby octopus while she glared at me was beyond satisfying.

"Sorry?" I chuckled before a wave of water struck me, courtesy of her noble steed.

Ian swam Meg over to the pier where she could sit and watch him get revenge for her.

Thus the second water fight of the season began, but there were no teams; it was every person for themselves. That lasted until Reyna and I decided to have some fun of our own. We took a deep breath and dove down to play a little game we liked to call Shark Bait.

Typically, we would circle around her brother, grazing his legs or arms or tickling his feet. Then we would latch onto his ankles and yank him under when he least expected it. Since there were two of them, we divided to conquer. I imagined Wesley would be the most fun since he had no idea what we were doing, but I let Reyna have him all to herself.

On the first circle around Ian, I brushed against his calf with my nails. His leg jerked in response and I narrowly dodged it as I circled him again. Just as I reached out to grab his ankle, I made the mistake of not striking from behind. Two hands curled around my arms and with a strong tug, I was pulled to the surface.

"Gotcha!" Ian shouted as he wrapped his arms around my waist. The victorious smile froze on his face when he realized how close we were, how different it was after the kiss.

Panting from holding my breath for so long underwater drew his gaze to the rise and fall of my chest pressed against his, but he averted his eyes almost immediately. I would have missed it if I wasn't paying attention.

Yet there was no missing it when he focused on my parted lips and lingered there.

He sounded distracted when he mumbled, "I caught a Ferra."

That snapped him out of it.

"Ferret!" He corrected in a hurry, "I caught a Ferret."

The nickname bothered me more than it should have because now he was using it to distance himself from me. It was like whenever he said it, I was no longer a girl he was attracted to, but just his sister's friend.

So I put my hands on his shoulders and pushed out of his arms, wanting that space as much as he seemed to want it too.

There was a moment of awkward silence before Wesley broke the surface of the water nearby, sputtering and gasping for air. Neither of us noticed Reyna pull him under, but their timing was impeccable. She came up a second later, gulping down oxygen when she wasn't laughing at her glowering boyfriend. He barely managed to keep a straight face before he lunged at her, taking her back under with him.

The water settled after a few seconds as we waited for them to resurface.

"What do you think they're doing?" Ian asked, inching closer to where they disappeared.

"Drowning in their love for each other," I snorted at my own pun.

"I was a lifeguard last year. There might be a casualty, but I can save one of them."

"Oh, leave them alone," I rolled my eyes, not wanting to put up with his overprotective behavior. "They'll be up for air soon."

Right after I said that, they floated back to the top, still kissing and unaware of us watching them.

Wesley broke their lip lock just before Ian pounced and I had to give him some credit for the delay. He wasn't going to hurt Wes, but they did take water fighting to another level. Reyna swam into the fray, complaining about leaving her out of it and vowing to protect her 'damn boyfriend' from the clutches of her 'stupid, evil brother.'

I was never one to be left out of a good fight. And I couldn't think of a better way to take out the tempestuous emotions brewing inside me than bitch-slapping the cause with a force of water.

Ian Winters didn't stand a chance against Hurricane Ferra.

So there was bloodshed during the fight...

...but it wasn't like I meant to make him bleed.

Honestly, it was Ian's fault for putting his nose in the path of my elbow. I told him that when we all swam back to shore so we could rest our limbs and have lunch.

"I think it's broken," he whined, gently touching his nose after he climbed onto the pier. "This is the second time. Why do you hate my nose so much?"

"It was an accident," I muttered. "And it's just a minor nosebleed."

To my left, Wesley pushed himself up out of the water too and held his hand out to Reyna. I watched as he pulled her out and couldn't hold my tongue when they both looked down at me, waiting on me to join them.

"What? You're not going to be a gentleman and help me too?" I winced at the unintended snark in my tone. I was in a mood, but they didn't deserve my wrath.

"I would," Wesley gave me a small smile while Reyna grinned, "but it looks like you already have someone to help you."

I turned my head to the right and only just took notice of the guy from earlier standing on the edge.

"Remind me to stay on your good side." He leaned over and reached his hand out to me. I graciously took it and let him help me out of the water. He flashed his boyish dimples, giving me a onceover and adding, "Even though I don't see any bad sides."

Laughter came easy with him. "There is no way you've had success with that one."

Reyna and Wesley walked off, the former looking at me like she expected details later. Ian hesitated as if he didn't want to leave, but then he turned and followed them back to the picnic table.

"You see," he picked up my clothes and handed the bundle to me, "now you have a special opportunity to prove yourself wrong."

"And why would I ever want to do that," I tilted my head with a smile, "when I prefer being right?"

"Reason number one, that was a great line. Reason number other one," he slid my shoes over to me so I could step into them, "because I would like to get to know you. And I think if you spend some time around me, I might get to see your real smile."

"I am smiling."

He pursed his lips, studying the upturned corners of my mouth and my eyes. Then he shook his head at what he found there, "Nope. That's not a real smile."

"And why do you say that, mystery man?"

"I have this friend who used to smile all the time to hide her real feelings. Usually it would be when she was irritated, and I'm not so good at telling the difference there, but..." He hesitated, shoving his thumbs into his pockets. "Sadness. That one is harder to hide."

I was speechless, caught off guard by his intuition.

"So Ferra," he tried after giving me a minute, "would like to go canoeing with me tomorrow afternoon?"

I bit my lip as I thought about my answer.

It would just be a harmless date with a guy I'd probably never see again.

Though I struggled with even the idea of a date when I had feelings for another guy, who confused the hell out of me.

There was no confusion involved with canoeing, especially with a cutie like the one waiting for my response.

I looked past him towards the table where Ian sat, eating a sandwich. He flinched when Meg poked his nose, and again when Reyna did it. I tried not to smile when he frowned at them and took another bite, his shoulders hunched as he sulked in pain.

The guy noticed where I was looking and said, "You don't have to answer now. I'll be here tomorrow and you can decide then if you want to hang out or not."

"I'd like that," I said, returning my full attention to him. I felt like the worst kind of person. "I would really like that—" I stopped. "Are you ever going to tell me your name?"

He chuckled, "Tomorrow, if you meet me here."

I sighed, giving him my best playful glare. "You're making your way to my bad side."

"Hey, I'll take any side you want to give me," he winked, chuckling again when I rolled my eyes. "Now I'm going to leave so you can eat and I can beat myself up over that last line. I'll admit it wasn't my best."

"You should definitely beat yourself up for that," I nodded, parting ways with him in favor of food. I was starving after going over twenty-four hours without a full meal.

"I'll throw an extra punch for you," he called out from behind me.

When I got to the table, I sat down across from the others. Our moms were sunbathing and reading, so they must have eaten without us. It was mostly quiet while I made my sandwich, until Ian cleared his throat.

"So what was that about punching?"

I took an aggressive bite of my food and responded with a dry stare.

He shrugged, picking at the chips on his plate, "I was just curious."

"What did the hottie want, sis?" Meg asked me next.

She was eating Skittles that I was positive my best friend supplied to her. Reyna had a handful of colorful candy poised to go in her mouth too. I raised a brow at her and didn't even have to say anything for her to get defensive.

"What?! It's not like I wanted to share," she grumbled dejectedly, separating the red ones in her cupped hand to save for last.

"It's fine," Meg huffed. "I'm allowed to have candy. Now tell us about the boy! Did he ask you on a date? Is he going to be your boyfriend? Did you kiss?"

Ian choked on his food when sugar-high Meg fired the last question. Reyna checked on him and he gave her a thumbs up to show that he wasn't dying. I waited until he was done to calmly answer what everyone at the table was wondering.

"He just asked if I want to go canoeing tomorrow."

Reyna threw a glance at Ian, gauging his reaction as she asked me, "Are you going to go?"

"Maybe? I don't know yet."

She saw that I was starting to get uncomfortable, so she came to my rescue by rambling on, "Who's excited for the scary stories tonight? I have a really good one to share. It's about a nightmare I had involving an apocalyptic world where Skittles were extinct and a mad scientist was to blame because he melted them all into a gooey rainbow that turned brown and murky."

"It's called a density rainbow," Wesley supplied. "And candy can be discontinued, but it can't be extinct."

"And that is why you were the villain in my nightmare," she shivered and asked me to hold her.

What she did was a reminder that she supported me as a friend more than her being the captain of the Fian ship. She would jump overboard and let it sink if I asked her to do it.

I wrapped my arm around her and gave her the hug we both needed.

12 | Campfire

2 | Campfire

~☁︎☀︎☁︎~

"To this day, he searches these woods for his next victim. He could be watching us now. Salivating as he anticipates tearing into his next living, breathing meal with his razor-sharp teeth and claws."

I rolled my eyes as Ian finished his scary story with bared teeth and wiggling fingers. Beside me, Reyna gave her brother a slow, hesitant clap of her hands as she chuckled nervously. It surprised me that she thought it was scary at all because it was just lame to me.

Megan was the one truly afraid. She was in tears and had her arms around Wesley's neck, strangling him for protection.

My parents were glaring at Ian for being insensitive to his younger audience, but they were the ones who gave into my sister's pleas of staying awake for the stories.

So much for being old enough to handle it.

"Your turn, Black!" Ian grinned at him from across the flames, the shadows creating a sinister feel to the curve of his mouth.

Meg screeched and buried her face in Wesley's neck.

"Um," Wes cleared his throat, discreetly attempting to loosen her grip on him, "I think I'll pass. You did such a good job scaring...everyone...I don't think I could compete with you."

"Aww, come on," Ian goaded, "It's not a competition."

"If it were, you would undoubtedly beat me."

Ian chuckled, "That's true, but—"

"I think we can all agree," my mom chimed in and went over to relieve Wesley of the monkey cutting off his air supply.

Ian's smile dropped into a frown as he looked at each of our expressions. The realization made him sheepish and he asked, "Was it that bad?"

We all confirmed it with nods and mumbled forms of 'yes,' so he slumped back in his chair.

"Sorry. I guess I got a little too into it. You ok, munchkin?"

Meg huffed, gaining some courage as she held onto our mom's hand, "I'm fine! If anyone is going to be eaten by a monster, it'll be you! You-you big meanie!"

"You're right," he was quick to agree. "I would deserve it too. And you're safe! You would be the last one he would go for because you're so small."

She gasped and he closed his eyes, his blabbering mistake occurring to him too late.

"Are you ok, hun?" His mom asked him as mine took Meg to bed.

"Yeah," he stood up and I almost missed his glance in my direction. "I'm just tired. It's been a long couple of days."

"Well, go get some sleep."

He said good night to everyone and I tilted my head as I watched him step into his tent. Even after he zipped it shut, I continued to stare and reflect on his behavior throughout the evening.

Ian was unusually quiet and distracted, but I tried not to jump to conclusions that I was the reason. If I wasn't struggling with my own thoughts about us or afraid of making it worse, I would have gone to check on him.

"If you ask me," Reyna whispered in my ear, "he's jealous of your date tomorrow."

"I don't recall asking you, Skit," I said, even though she voiced my own assumption. "And it's not a date."

"Not-date then," she winked, "but we know how those turn out."

I tossed my lap blanket over her head, letting out a laugh as she flailed around underneath it. It served her right, but I loved her enough to help her come out for air when she got tangled up in it.

We stayed around the campfire for a while longer until the last of us were ready to go to sleep. My dad smothered the fire, so we only had the moonlight to guide the path to our tents. Wesley was unfortunate enough to be tent buddies with Ian, while Reyna and I had to share with Megan.

She stayed asleep as we snuck inside and fumbled in the dark to change into our pajamas. She didn't even wake up when we slipped into our sleeping bags on either side of her.

No, it had to be about an hour after we fell asleep.

I swore it was a little sister superpower of hers, along with her strength to shake me awake.

"Ferra," she whined. Then she gave Reyna the same treatment.

"What's wrong, Sunshine?" My friend asked her groggily while I groaned and rolled over to face her too.

"I had a nightmare and now I'm scared and can't go back to sleep."

Stifling a yawn, I tried to be a good older sister and provide some comfort. I offered what worked in the past whenever she had a nightmare, "Want to try counting unicorns?"

"I'm too old for that now," she said, her indignation still intact in times of trouble. "I want Sir Cuddleton."

"Who's that? Your bear?"

She shook her head, "Wesley. He's my knight, so he can protect me while I sleep."

I looked over at Reyna who just shrugged.

"I guess we can ask if you can stay with him."

"No! I don't want to be in there with Ian. He's a jerk and it's his fault I had a nightmare."

"I don't know what you want me to do then, Meg," I rubbed my tired eyes.

"Go get him. He can sleep in here."

I motioned around the tent, "There's not space in here for another person."

"Then I guess I won't get my beautiful sleep tonight."

I didn't correct her for once because sleep was beautiful.

No sleep was an ugly, ugly thing and she was implying that she wouldn't let us get any tonight.

Reyna could see my frustration, so she suggested, "Wes could stay just until you fall asleep. Would that be ok, Sunshine?"

Meg nodded, "Ok, Reyny Day."

"And where are we supposed to go in the meantime?" I questioned.

Reyna's smile turned into a grimace, "I was going to stay here with her."

And Wesley, she failed to include.

"Maybe you could stay in their tent for a little while? Ian sleeps like a log, so I doubt he'll even notice you're there."

Too tired to care, I heaved a sigh and got to my feet. Wrapping a blanket around my shoulders, I made a point to mention how much I hated them and continued to grumble my complaints all the way to the boys' tent. I couldn't exactly knock, so I quietly unzipped the tent and peeked inside.

The two of them were on opposite ends of the tent with a gap between their sleeping bags, as if they couldn't stand to be near each other. I identified Wesley's dark head of hair and reached in to tap his foot. He didn't wake up, so I tapped harder.

Still nothing.

Reyna should have been the one to retrieve her boyfriend. I mouthed a curse at him and crawled into the space, careful not to brush against either boy. Taking a lesson from my sister, I shook him aggressively and whispered his name.

He jolted awake, squinting in the darkness at me while he blindly reached for his glasses. Once they were on, he blinked as his eyes adjusted. "Ferra? What's wrong? Is Reyna ok?"

I shushed him, glancing over my shoulder when Ian shifted onto his back to check if he was still asleep.

"She's fine," I assured Wesley under my breath after Ian stopped moving. "Meg had a nightmare. She wants to know if you can stay with her until she falls asleep."

"Yeah, I can do that," he sat up and yawned.

"You don't mind?"

"Of course not," he smiled as he tried to smooth out his bed head. He looked from me to Ian and back, "You're welcome to sleep here in the meantime."

I thanked him, hoping to get some rest away from the bugs and dark forest. After he left, I laid down where I was since it would have been weird to use his sleeping bag. There was no cushion for my head, but it was still better than being outside without any shelter.

I settled in under my blanket and closed my eyes.

"Ferra?"

Well crap.

Maybe if I pretend to be asleep.

I steadied my breathing and held completely still.

Asleep, not dead.

I forced my body to relax and as I debated on snoring, I heard him turn onto his side.

"I know you're awake. I heard everything."

"Sorry for not being quieter," I mumbled with my eyes still shut.

"It's alright. I couldn't sleep anyway."

I didn't respond.

"You don't look very comfortable over there."

Thanks for noticing, I thought, shifting when I felt a rock dig into my back. "I'm fine."

"Liar," he called me out just above a whisper. "Come here. We already shared a sleeping bag once. We can do it again."

"That was for survival."

"Our circumstances weren't that dire, so please stop making excuses and come over here. I just want you off the cold, hard ground."

I could have argued.

In fact, I wanted to argue.

Maybe I did it because I knew it would never happen again. I would be ok with letting him go if I got to be in his arms one more time.

Or I hoped he wouldn't want to let go of me.

It was pathetic, but I allowed myself to indulge anyway.

I shoved my blanket aside and scooted over to his side while he unzipped the bag, holding it open for me to slide in with him.

Ian reached over me to pull the zipper back up and he breathed by my ear, "Better?"

"Yeah, thanks."

He was keeping as much respectable distance as he could in the confined space. There were a couple of inches between us, but I could still feel the warmth radiating from him.

"Ian?"

He hummed in response.

"You seemed off tonight. Are you ok?"

There was a long pause and I thought he fell asleep.

"Yes. No." Then he murmured, "I don't know."

I waited for him to say more, but after a minute or two of silence, I felt a hesitant touch on my waist. He turned me onto my back and sat up on his elbow to look down at me.

He looked me in the eye, his hand still on my waist when he asked, "Are you going to meet up with that guy tomorrow?"

"I haven't decided yet," I answered truthfully, "but I don't have a reason not to do it. Do I?"

His brows lowered as he considered my words, unsure what to do with them.

Now or never.

"Give me a reason."

We were close enough now that I could feel when his breath caught. "Ferra—"

I knew he was going to try being the voice of reason instead of taking action, so I repeated what he said to me and gave it a new meaning.

"Stop making excuses and come here."

Ian's slack jaw clenched and his gaze danced across my face, lingering on the smile that curved my lips. His hand on my waist slid down to my hip as he moved in closer, resting his forehead on mine. My eyes drifted shut when the careful weight of his body pressed against mine and he exhaled softly, our lips only centimeters apart.

Then he tensed.

His breath hitched again, but not in a good way. It was like he snapped out of a daze and realized what he was about to do.

Hissing a curse, he pushed away from me and rolled onto his back. "I can't do this, Ferra."

Shock coursed through my veins like cold ice, but it quickly gave way to fiery anger.

"Why?" I forced out, but he didn't respond to me. I yanked on the zipper of the sleeping bag so I could sit up and stare down at him, "I'm sick of your mixed signals. The least you can do is tell me why!"

"I'm sorry."

As soon as those two familiar words left his mouth, I grabbed my blanket and stood up. Being outside with the bugs was infinitely better than staying sheltered with him.

"Please don't run again, Ferra."

I thought he was trying to stop me because he was ready to talk, so I paused to hear him out.

Then he said, "I don't want you to get hurt."

Whether he was talking about a bear mauling me or suffering a broken heart, I scoffed with my back to him. Before I stepped outside, I said, "Don't worry. I'm not leaving the campsite...I'm just leaving you."

After I sealed the tent, I wrapped my blanket around my shoulders and went over to the charred remains of the fire to sit. I buried my face in the blanket and tried not to cry because he wasn't worth any more tears.

A rustling sound startled me and I didn't know which would be worse; a bear or Ian.

It was only Wesley coming out. He jumped too when he turned around and saw me sitting outside, blinking wide-eyed at him like an owl.

He walked over and sit in the chair beside mine. "I wasn't expecting you to be out here. Everything ok?"

I bit my lip, ready to pretend it was, but I shook my head.

Wesley glanced towards the tent, "Is he being dumb again?"

I laughed softly. Bitterly. "Yeah, you could say that..."

"I'm surprised that you like him."

I was caught off guard by his bold statement. Though it was a strange subject to discuss with my best friend's boyfriend, talking about it with someone else was better than wallowing in bitter silence.

"Why is it surprising?"

Wesley showed his first sign of discomfort by adjusting his glasses. It was after all our first time talking one-on-one and what a way to start. "He's a good guy," he hesitated to continue, perhaps afraid of offending me, "but he can be immature."

I readily agreed, "my sister acts older than him half the time."

"My point is, you and I don't know each other that well, but it doesn't seem like a trait that you would find endearing."

"People are a lot more complex than any of your science experiments, Wesley."

"I know that now, but I still revert to my old ways on occasion."

I chuckled halfheartedly, dropping my gaze to my fiddling hands on my lap. "Ian is mature when he needs to be—when it matters the most."

Wesley may not have been a good people person, but he knew I had more to say and gave me the time I needed to continue.

"He had to grow up fast when his dad left. More like he wanted to do it, so he could be there for his mom and sister. Whenever I hung out with Reyna, she and I would get so annoyed with him when he would boss us around like he was much older."

I smiled at the memories that have become oddly precious to me.

"He pulled stupid pranks in school or on the two of us. He'd whine when he didn't get his way. And he still acts so beyond dejected when Reyna gets mad at him.

"But whenever she was sick, he skipped school to take care of her. He would choose being home with his family or babysitting Reyna over hanging out with his own friends. Did you know he's amazing at math?"

"Really?" The disbelief was clear in Wesley's quiet tone.

"Yep. He wanted to help his mom with the bills and finances, even though she didn't need him to do it. He's a lot smarter than he lets on. He also likes to box, and he learned self-defense just so he could teach Reyna a few moves..." I trailed off from rambling about him and just shrugged, "He's pretty incredible."

"Wow," Wesley said when he was sure I was done talking.

I nodded.

"You must really love him."

My heart jumped to my throat as I blankly stared at Wesley.

Love him?

I never thought of it as more than 'like,' but when the word 'love' was said so blatantly and out loud, something clicked in my mind. I had known Ian for years—I practically grew up with him—and it only just became apparent that my feelings grew with me. It was beyond a mere crush or simply liking him.

I swallowed the sob fighting to break free, but I couldn't stop a few hopeless tears from escaping. It was so unlike me, but I didn't know what to do. Fully aware of how deep my feelings went now, I could almost feel my heart breaking in two when I thought of his rejections.

"What do I do now?"

Wesley offered a kind, sympathetic smile, "I think Reyna would have to help you with that one."

"I already know what she would say because it's the same thing I would say to her."

"And what would that be?"

"She would tell me to fight for him, tell him how I feel. If he doesn't feel the same way, then at least I won't be wondering and I can move on."

"It's good advice," he commented.

"It would be nice to have a guy's perspective." And an easier option. "Can you try?"

"You really want my opinion? You might not like it."

"Yes," I pulled the blanket tighter around me, bracing myself for the cold, hard truth.

"If he already rejected you, telling him how you feel might only hurt you more in the end. Stop waiting for Ian to make up his mind because you could be waiting a long time. Find someone else who deserves your love." He stood up and grinned, "Canoeing on a lake is a good place to start."

He said good night to me and was only a few steps away when I softly called out to him. He looked back over his shoulder.

"That wasn't reverse psychology, was it?"

"Chemistry is my expertise," he said with a smirk, "not psychology."

I didn't quite believe him, but I liked his advice more than my own. Not telling Ian how I felt was the easy way out, but there was nothing wrong with that...right?

13 | canoe

1 3 | Canoe

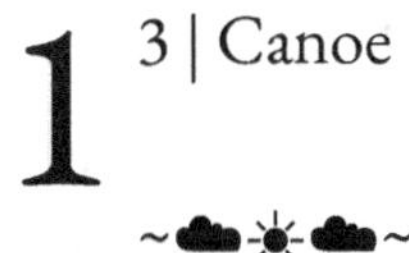

On the walk to the lake, my arm was hooked through Reyna's and my feet were dragging. She knew something was wrong and it was easy to figure out who caused my sullen mood, but she didn't broach the subject. Instead, she gave me her shoulder to lean on even though she was shorter than me and it was uncomfortable to walk that way.

I stared straight ahead, ignoring the presence behind us. We led the group, and Ian was in the back alone because my little sister didn't want to have anything to do with him either. He tried to talk to me twice earlier in the morning, but I refused to give him a chance to apologize.

Once we reached the lake, Reyna started to pull me away from the group, but then she halted with a gasp.

"Oh my god. Is that Mr. F?!" She pointed to a man sitting in a chair near the water.

Her loud voice startled the man and he nearly dropped the fishing pole from his hands. After the shock of seeing us so far from home wore off, he heaved a sigh before giving us a tight smile and a wave.

Yep, that was definitely our chemistry teacher.

Mr. Fredrick gave Reyna a chance to pass his class when she was failing, which ultimately brought her and Wesley together. I liked to think of him as the captain of their ship, and he was a decent teacher too.

Reyan and I went over to greet him.

"What a...nice surprise seeing you all here," he said, nodding to Wesley and Ian as they joined us.

"What brings you here, Mr. F?" Reyna asked him.

"Peace," he responded too quickly. Then he coughed and said more calmly, "I came here for some peace and quiet."

"It is nice out here," Theresa, Reyna and Ian's mom, commented as she stepped up behind us.

"Yes," he agreed with her. "It certainly was—is nice out here. Away from," he glanced at us teens, "civilization."

I snorted and Reyna looked at me with a grin of her own. Even if he did care for his students, he must have been less than thrilled to see some of us during summer vacation. I would hate it if I were in his position.

"Come on, everyone," Theresa said, "I'm sure Mr. Fredrick would like to be alone."

She had a knowing smile on her face that he warmed up to and returned to her.

"I don't mind, really," he said, a layer of sweetness in his tone I had never heard in the classroom. "I'm just a little out of my element, seeing people I know out here."

Reyna perked up, "Was that a chemistry pun?"

Wesley shook his head, "Wrong kind of element."

"It's always a pleasure to see my two favorite students," he chuckled at the two of them.

"Hey," I chimed in, "what about me?"

"And me!" Ian added, sharing an awkward look with me.

Ian was one of Mr. Fredrick's students before he graduated last year. And with the final prank he pulled on the teachers, I imagined that he wasn't high on the list of favorite students for any of them.

"You two are alright," he said with a noncommittal shrug of a shoulder.

I pretended to take offense by saying, "Well, in that case... It was nice seeing you Mr. Fredrick, but there is important fun to be had elsewhere for us younger folk."

He raised his brows, "What a subtle way of saying that I'm old, Ms. Chandler."

"I appreciate your subtle way of leaving me out of that statement," Theresa noted with a soft....giggle?

"That's right," Reyna raised her voice, garnering everyone's attention as she turned to me. "You don't want to keep your date waiting, Fere."

She weaved her arm through mine again and started walking away.

"You realize they were flirting, right?" I said under my breath, smirking when she wrinkled her nose.

"They were just getting along. That's all."

I nodded, "Right. Getting along."

Ian's voice grated on my nerves when he called out, "Ferra!"

It was my turn to stop, causing Reyna to stumble back a step. I thought it would be better to shut him down now than deal with it all day.

"Holy crap," my friend whispered when we turned around and saw Ian jogging over. "He didn't call you Ferret. This must be serious."

Then she wandered off with the excuse of needing to save Wesley from the clutches of my little sister.

"We need to talk," Ian said when he reached me.

"No, we don't."

"Yes, we do. I have to—"

"No, you don't," I cut him off. "You don't have to say anything, Ian. I need time."

"Please, just let me—"

I stepped around him and hurried to create some distance between us. If I heard him say another word, I would break down and I wouldn't let him see me cry. It was petty of me to not let him talk—and I had a nagging curiosity about what he had to say—but to protect my heart and pride, I couldn't hear him out.

Reyna and I spent the rest of the early afternoon soaking up the sun together. Wesley stayed with us for a while, but when Reyna gave him a signal that she thought I wouldn't see, he excused himself to go get a drink. A few minutes later, I looked over to see him preoccupied with a giggling Megan.

"Don't let my brother ruin this trip for you," my bestie announced.

"Ok, we're just diving right in then."

My eyes were drawn to the subject of our new conversation. Ian had been attempting to fish with Mr. Fredrick and my dad for a while now, but all he succeeded in was annoying them. From where we watched, we gathered that he somehow managed to tangle his line with Mr. Fredrick's and he made my dad miss out on a big fish.

"Ian is stupid and you're amazing," Reyna said after scowling at her brother.

"Well, I already knew that..."

"Do I think you should talk to him and tell him how you feel? Yes, part of me does think you need to do it."

I rolled my eyes, but then what she said next surprised me.

"Do I also think he should suffer first and reflect on his idiotic ways? Hell yes."

"You do?"

"And you, my dear friend, need to have some fun," she continued as if I hadn't spoken. "There is a nice, charming, hot guy down by the lake that wants to spend time with you and appreciates a damn fine catch when he sees one."

Fine catch, I thought as I looked back over at Ian. I needed to stop taking the bait and it would be his loss if he didn't want me in the end.

There are plenty of other fish in the sea for this beautiful bass.

I was going to take Reyna and Wesley's advice. I needed to enjoy what was left of our camping trip and put the drama behind me. For now, anyway. I wasn't the type to run from my problems, no matter how tempting it was to do so. Although, that didn't mean I couldn't take the scenic route to facing those problems.

Giving it no more thought, I stood up and said, "You're right, Skit."

It was time to go canoeing with a cutie.

He was sitting on the ground near the canoe, looking out at the lake with a soft smile on his face. He turned at the sound of rocks shifting under my feet, squinting to see who was approaching and smiled when he saw it was me.

"I didn't think you were going to come," he grinned as he rose to his feet.

"My curiosity to know the name of the boy who shamelessly flirted with me was just too much to bear," I told him with a wistful sigh. "Unless you want me to remember you as 'Dimples' for the rest of my life."

He laughed, showing them off and making me smile. "I wouldn't mind that, but far be it from me to let you live your whole life wondering."

"Well? What is it?"

"Impatient," he tsked. "My name is Eli."

"Eli," I tested his name out. "I think I prefer Dimples. It suits you."

"I'm okay with that," he winked. Then in a sweeping motion, he gestured to the canoe, "Shall we?"

I took his hand with a grateful smile, only hesitating a moment when the urge to look back where I came from struck me. I was determined to enjoy myself and his company, so I kept my eyes ahead of me.

We settled in across from each other and Eli started paddling once he made sure that I was ready to go.

It was a beautiful day. The steady sound of the paddles wading through the water filled our companionable silence, washing away my troubles with each stroke. I watched the trees surrounding us sway in a soft breeze, a sigh of content releasing from my lungs. Then I tilted my head back, closed my eyes, and soaked up the warmth of the sun.

"You look like you needed this," he said.

I opened my eyes, only just noticing that we weren't moving anymore and we were out towards the middle of the lake.

"Yeah," I gave him a grateful smile. "I needed to escape for a little while."

"Escape?" A cute wrinkle formed between his brows. "You shouldn't have to escape anything on vacation."

"Other than younger siblings," I half-joked.

He chuckled, nodding in agreement. "The one exception. Or in my case, two little brothers."

"Ouch," I grimaced for him. "So do you have any plans this summer that don't involve them?"

"Is that an invitation?" He teased with an infectious grin before giving his answer. "If all goes according to plan, I'll be far away from them for a couple of weeks. My cousins own a beach house, so I'm going to visit them. The best part is that I get to drive all the way there. Just me and the open road."

"Do you like driving?"

"I love it. It's like breathing to me."

I smiled because I could relate; that was the way I felt about dancing.

"What about you? Any escape plans?"

I was almost tempted to ask if that was an invitation from him, but I wouldn't go on a road trip with someone I barely knew. Even if it was better than the alternative, because my summer was turning into a real bummer.

"I wish," I admitted.

"It can't be that hard to get away from a little kid," he said, looking off into the distance. Then with a hint of a smirk, he trailed off, "Unless..."

"Unless?"

His eyes met mine again, twinkling and knowing, "Unless you're trying to escape someone else."

I squinted at him, "How do you do that?"

"What?"

"We've just met, but you seem to know...I don't know. Everything."

He laughed, "Oh, I don't know everything. I'm just observant and good at reading people."

"So you read me like an open book," I stated more than questioned.

"No, just a few pages. Your, uh, friend though...he's like an audio-book at max volume."

A burst of laughter bubbled up from my throat, "I must be deaf then."

His attention went past my shoulder again, "Or maybe you just need to listen more closely?"

I followed his line of sight. We drifted towards the shore while we were talking, so we were only about thirty or so feet from the dock. I swung my head back around when I thought I met Ian's gaze. Even from a distance, it was painfully obvious that he was watching us.

"He's just being protective. It's all he seems to know how to do."

"Not true. I've seen that look before, when my best friend thought I was hitting on the girl he was crazy about... In my defense, it was intentional to push him into making a move."

"That's a completely different situation."

Mischief extended the curve of his lips and lifted his brows, "Wanna bet?"

My eyes narrowed and I crossed my arms, "No."

"You want to know how he feels about you, right?"

After a moment, I begrudgingly nodded.

"Will you take a chance on a handsome stranger with the most adorable dimples you've ever seen?"

"Who also happens to be a matchmaker?"

"I should start charging for my services, but for you? No charge. So," he smiled, "what do you think?"

"I don't know..."

"Now's the time, beautiful." He glanced behind me again. "While he's watching us."

I took a breath and asked, "What do we do?"

"The angle should be just right," Eli scanned the canoe and our position.

Then he took my hands in his and coaxed me forward, moving our hands out and entwining our fingers. "Okay so far?"

"Yeah, but I don't get how this is going to—"

"Shh," he leaned in, meeting me in the middle. "Tilt your head to the left, just a little."

I did as he said, wondering if he was going to try to kiss me. We were only a couple of inches away, but he didn't move. My heart sped up at our proximity and the intensity of his gaze, but there was no real depth to it; just a natural reaction to having a cute boy's undivided attention.

"Still ok?" He whispered.

"You're going to make a girl very lucky someday, you know that?"

"Why, thank you," he murmured with a smile, abandoning my hands to move his own up to my hair. His fingers tangled loosely in the strands at the back of my head as he tilted it more, like one would do to deepen a kiss.

In doing that, he was able to see in Ian's direction again and he chuckled, clearly satisfied with what he saw. His arms fell away and he scooted back to his spot. I gave him a strange look as he grasped the paddles and started moving to the dock.

"That's it?"

A single brow rose, "Did you want a real kiss? I'd be happy to oblige, but I think you'd rather get it from him."

"It can't be that simple!"

"Speaking as a male myself, I can tell you that we're very simple creatures. It just takes the right thing to trigger our more," he searched for the right words, "primal instincts?"

There was a soft thud when we bumped into the dock. We made it there awfully quick and I wasn't even close to being prepared for what I was about to face.

My eyes widened at Eli, but he just winked at me.

"It was a pleasure, Ferra."

A shadow fell over us, blocking the sunlight. I looked up at Ian, but his impassive expression told me nothing as he silently held his hand out to me.

I spent most of the day avoiding him, but I couldn't turn away now. I put my hand in his and he squeezed it, the tension in his shoulders only relaxing by a fraction at my touch.

With a last glance at Eli and his dimples on full display, I was carefully pulled up and out of the canoe by Ian, who acted as if the other boy wasn't even there.

And as soon as my feet touched the wooden dock, Ian ducked down to lift me and throw me over his shoulder.

I didn't think Ian would take the 'primal instinct' thing that far.

My voice rang out, "Put me down, you neanderthal!"

"No," he muttered gruffly, hoisting me higher before he started walking towards the trees.